The Position of Peggy Harper

The Position of Peggy Harper

Leonard Merrick

Foreword by George Orwell

Published by Hesperus Press Limited
28 Mortimer Street, London W1W 7RD
www.hesperuspress.com

The Position of Peggy Harper first published in 1911
First published by Hesperus Press Limited, 2013

Foreword by George Orwell (Copyright © George Orwell, 1945) by
permission of Bill Hamilton as the Literary Executor of the Estate of the
Late Sonia Brownell Orwell and Secker & Warburg Ltd.

Designed and typeset by Fraser Muggeridge studio
Printed and bound in Italy by Grafica Veneta

ISBN: 978-184391-385-6

CONTENTS

Leonard Merrick died in 1939, but during the later part of his life wrote, or at any rate published, nothing but short stories. Except for one early and now forgotten book, *Violet Moses*, his full-length novels all belong to the period between 1900 and 1914. There are about a dozen of them in all, and their general level is so high that though it would be fairly easy to pick out six of them as being better worth reprinting than the rest, it is not easy to narrow the choice down to a single volume.

Merrick has the peculiarity that, though he is by no means a 'highbrow' writer, the background of his stories is almost invariably one or other of the arts. Among his full-length novels, the only exceptions to this rule are *The Worldlings*, a story of imposture founded on the Tichborne case, and *One Man's View*, which is a partial exception in so much that the central character is a lawyer. Otherwise the people he habitually writes about are novelists, poets, painters and, most characteristically of all, actors. If there is one thing above all others for which he deserves to be remembered, it is his extraordinarily convincing and glamourless picture of stage life; and this, perhaps, justifies the reprinting of *The Position of Peggy Harper* rather than of, say, *Cynthia* or *The Worldlings*, which are equally good in their different way.

Although nearly all of Merrick's books are about writers or artists, they can be divided fairly sharply into two classes. One class, by which unfortunately he is best known, are his Paris books, mostly collections of short stories, such as *A Chair on the Boulevard*. These stories describe a kind of Bohemianism which Merrick had not experienced from the inside and which only doubtfully exists; the atmosphere they are trying to reproduce is that of *Trilby* or even, at their worst, that of W.J. Locke's *Aristide Pujol*. Where Merrick describes *his own* adventures in Paris, as he obviously does in certain chapters in *Cynthia*, for instance, it is quite a different story. Picturesqueness disappears, and in its place there enters that dreadful thing which he understood so well, poverty against a background of gentility. Merrick's shabby-genteel novels are the ones that matter: the best of them, apart from those that have been mentioned already, are *The Man Who Was Good*,

The Actor Manager, The House of Lynch and *The Quaint Companions.*
Conrad in Quest of His Youth, one of Merrick's most successful books,
deals partly with stage life, but differs from the others in that poverty is
not a leading theme in it.

Money is always a fascinating subject, provided that only small
sums are involved. Brute starvation is not interesting, and neither are
transactions involving thousands of millions of pounds; but an out-of-
work actor pawning his watch-chain and wondering whether next week
the watch will have to follow it – that is interesting. However, Merrick's
books are not simply concerned with the difficulty of making a living.
His theme is rather the humiliation which a sensitive and honest person
feels when he is forced into contact with people whose standards
are commercial. Christopher Tatham, the hero of *Peggy Harper,* writes
a melodrama which scores a thunderous success while the comedies
into which he has put his real work grow dog-eared on their journey
from agent to agent. It is an interesting detail – a reminder that, after all,
the status of the literary man *has* risen during the past thirty or forty
years –that the sum Tatham receives for his five-act melodrama is fifteen
pounds! But the fact that he is underpaid is socially less significant than
the fact that he is isolated.

Until it is almost too late, he simply does not have the opportunity
of making contact with people in any way similar to himself. His silly,
snobbish mother, and his prosperous uncle who is 'associated with
hops', are somewhat further from understanding his point of view than
the vulgar actor-manager who buys his melodrama. The foolish engagement into which he enters is the direct result of isolation. When he first
meets Peggy Harper, at the age of twenty-one or thereabouts, he probably does not know – never having had the chance to find out – that
there exist women who are both attractive and intelligent. Until he has
made his mark by individual effort, society has no place for him. The
dull commercial world of his family and the vulgar, down-at-heel world
of the touring companies are equally hostile to him, and it is largely luck
that the one or the other does not swallow him up for good.

Merrick is not consciously, or at any rate not overtly, a 'writer with a
purpose'. The commercialism and philistinism of the English-speaking
civilisation is something that he inveighs against but assumes to be

unchangeable, like the English climate. And there are many of the accepted values of his time that he does not even question. In particular, he everywhere takes for granted the superiority of a 'gentleman' to a 'bounder' and of a 'good accent' to cockney; and in most of his books there are passages which if they were written today would be called snobbish. Actually, Merrick is not a snobbish writer – if he were he would probably write about wealthy or titled people instead of concentrating on the shabby-genteel – but he is too honest to disguise his instinctive preferences. He feels strongly that good manners and delicate sensibilities are important, and that one of the worst horrors of poverty is having to take orders from ill-bred, coarse-fibred people. A beautiful little scene in *Peggy Harper* illustrates the kind of servitude that an educated man in a low-class touring company must be ready to put up with. The word 'menace' has occurred in the script of the play that is being rehearsed, and the ignoramus of a stage manager insists that it should be pronounced 'manace':

'What's that – what d'ye call it? "Menace?" Rats! That's extant, that's altogether extant.' He evidently relished his discovery of 'extant', which he seemed to believe was a scholarly synonym for 'out of date'. He looked round for Tatham. 'Isn't "menace" extant, eh?' he enquired.

'Quite,' said Tatham.

Peggy Harper, like most of Merrick's books (the outstanding exception is *The Man Who Was Good),* has a 'happy ending', but it is implied all the way through that decency and intelligence are very serious handicaps. In *Cynthia,* which is a story about a novelist, the clash between honesty and bread and butter is even more painful.

Cynthia is a book which it would not be altogether absurd to mention in the same sentence as George Gissing's *New Grub Street,* but its theme is one that a good many different writers have handled. The special thing that Merrick could do, and which no one else seems to have done, is to reproduce the atmosphere of low-class theatrical life: the smell of greasepaint and fish and chips, the sordid rivalries, the comfortless Sunday journeys, the lugging of suitcases through the back streets of unfamiliar towns, the 'professional' lodgings presided over by 'Ma', the poky bedrooms with the rickety washhand-stand and the grim white chamber-pot under the bed (does Merrick ever mention the chamber-pot? Probably not: one just seems to imagine it), and the trudging up and down the Strand on worn-out boot-soles, the agents' offices where women in dyed frocks sit waiting their turn, the forlorn collection of press cuttings, the manager who bolts in the middle of the tour with all the takings.

Although Merrick was fairly successful, especially towards the end of his life, as a short-story writer, his full-length novels never 'sold' in this country. About 1918 Messrs Hodder and Stoughton issued a uniform edition of his works with introductions by H.G. Wells, G.K. Chesterton, W.D. Howells and other well-known writers who admired him and felt that he was underrated. The introduction to *Peggy Harper* was written by Sir Arthur Pinero. The uniform edition, however, was no more successful than earlier editions had been – a fact which is all the more puzzling because throughout his life Merrick's books sold relatively well in the United States. The obvious explanation of his unpopularity is that he chose to write about artists, whereas the big public, as he himself often remarked, would sooner read about politicians or businessmen; also that his books are what people call 'grey', or 'gloomy', or 'too like real life'. It is quite true that the majority of Merrick's books are far from

Being cheer-up stories. They are lightly written, and for the sake of preserving the comedy form they usually have a 'happy ending', but their underlying mood is a bitter one. But it is still not clear why Merrick should have been more popular in America. The American public is presumably no more inclined than the British to take sides with the artist against society: nor did Merrick make any special concessions to American readers, for the subject-matter and the whole atmosphere of most of his books are intensely English.

Possibly, from the American point of view, the Englishness was an exotic attraction, while the kind of poverty and failure that Merrick was describing were not quite the kind that Americans are afraid of. At any rate, Merrick's steady refusal to see silver linings where none existed must have had something to do with his unpopularity. It is perhaps significant that *Conrad in Quest of His Youth,* the hero of which is wealthy, was about the most successful of his books. Now that the fear of poverty is a less urgent emotion, and the demand for sunshine stories less insistent, he seems overdue for revival.

– George Orwell, 1945

(Written [late 1945] for Eyre and Spottiswoode who wanted to publish a reprint of *The Position of Peggy Harper* with this introduction. The book, however, was never published.)

The Position of Peggy Harper

BOOK I

I

A gentleman who had been called to the Bar, expecting to make a great name and a large fortune, died obscurely, leaving the sum of £57 3s. 6d., a widow, and a son. His other surviving relative was a married sister. This lady said to her husband, who was lucratively associated with hops, 'You had better find a berth for Christopher in the office, George.'

Christopher Tatham had come down abruptly from Oxford, where George Spaulding and his wife, not unreasonably, considered that it was preposterous to have sent him, and had seemed to view his proposed introduction to the office in a proper light. Then, in a burst of confidence one day, he avowed to his aunt that, from his childhood, he had been ambitious to go on the stage. And he did not go into the office. 'Uncle George' had an open mind, and sons of his own to share the profits of hops, and he said, 'Well, if he has any talent that way, the best thing he can do is to become an actor – there's no future for him in the business, you know. Tell him to come and stay with us while he looks round.'

The process of looking round, as conducted by a novice, led to nothing but fruitless interviews with needy persons who advertised for 'Amateurs of ability' and sought simpletons of means, but Mr Spaulding occasionally met footlight favourites at Masonic dinners, and generously he proceeded to make himself a nuisance to them. 'A young protégé of mine, who is an aspirant for histrionic honours' figured in his discourse so often that several theatrical celebrities grew profane when they found they were to sit next to him. His persistence at last secured a chance for Tatham to make his debut at a fashionable theatre as an 'extra gentle-man' – in which capacity he received a guinea a week, and his principal duty was to simulate enjoyment of an imitation ice-cream composed of pink cotton-wool. 'Extra gentlemen' are supernumeraries of some refinement, who possess dress-clothes of their own and don't look like waiters when they are meant to represent Lady Alethea's guests. The widow, meanwhile, had been living in a boarding-house on the balance of the £57 3s. 6d. Her son took fifteen shillings of his salary to her every Sunday and continued to be sheltered by the Spauldings.

The career of the comedy was discomfitingly brief, and the one that followed it extended no hospitality to 'guests'. But after an anxious interval, the aspirant obtained an opportunity – thanks to Masonic dinners again – to play small parts, at small terms, in a stock company in the East End. His first appearance there was made as 'Ginger Bill' in *The Romany Rye*, and when he put on the corduroys, and the carroty wig that didn't fit him, the evil heat of the dressing room and the smell of the other actors' fried fish and chips intensified the sickness of his terror.

However, his performance of a hooligan gave satisfaction, though he had amused the East End company at rehearsal by having to inquire the meaning of the word 'barney' in his part. The audience paid him the compliment of calling him before the curtain in the role of 'Ginger Bill'. They approved him moderately in various roles that he sustained during the season. And then, one red-letter night, a provincial actress, who had come to the theatre to star in a sensational drama of her own composition, offered him an engagement to tour in it.

It was a testimonial. There was jealousy. 'She'd have liked to get *me*,' declared a favourite of Whitechapel, devouring his pen'orth of fried fish, 'but she said, "I know what it is – you London actors won't leave town!"' In the new engagement, the weekly salary was a couple of pounds, and the young man contrived to remit a sovereign each week now to his mother. It was progress. It was felt that 'Christopher was beginning to get on.' Only, when the tour terminated, he was, naturally, again without money to live on while he waited for the next.

Of course, his uncle and aunt understood the circumstances, and he was told to remember that he had a 'home to go to'. He was told to remember it on subsequent occasions. But actors in their novitiate, without theatrical families to smooth their path, need a home to go to very often, and Tatham, who was denied the possibility of saving anything while an engagement lasted, needed one even oftener than most of them. As time went on, the Spauldings did not actually con-clude that he had been misled by vanity and hadn't any aptitude for acting, but they sighed that it was 'strange he didn't do better'; they did not say bluntly that he was 'to blame', but they said disparagingly 'he was unlucky'. It began to be obvious to them that a young man who had a mother to support would, after all, be more suitably employed in a permanent clerkship than in a precarious profession. And their nephew became acutely conscious of their view.

He was acutely conscious of it this evening. Another third-rate tour had reached its last night, and tomorrow he would have to present himself at Regent's Park once more. He sickened to think of it. He was performing a part devoid of human nature, in a melodrama that outraged possibilities, to an audience for whom it was fully good enough; but he had looked forward to better things, and his heart was in his calling, though its apprenticeship was foul. Sentiment possessed him as he spoke the final lines of the balderdash and left the stage, wondering whether he would ever stand upon a stage again. Envy of the other men assailed him, untalented and unambitious as he knew most of them to be – at least they belonged to 'the profession'. It was their destiny, while his own foothold in it was so insecure. Yes, he had always felt it to be insecure. Even across his brightest moments had rolled the misgiving,

'Will it last?'

'Galbraith,' he said in the dressing room, to a tall, spare man seated before a looking glass, 'how did you find engagements at the start – before people had heard of you?'

Mr Galbraith, who was habited as a parson, and had still to play in two scenes, was smoking a pipe, while he dabbed chalk on his hair to betoken anguish induced by a prodigal son. He was a man of education, who had once been a West End actor. His descent was due to drink, a vice which he solemnly renounced as often as compassion entrusted him with another chance to earn his bread. For weeks and sometimes months at a stretch he would be a total abstainer, proclaiming barley-water his beverage for life – only to succumb, in his most confident hour, and be dismissed abusively from one company more. He remained in this one because, when his outbreak occurred, the tour had been so near its end that the manager had shirked the trouble of replacing him, but the spectacle of an intoxicated parson exhorting his son to reformation had injured the week's receipts.

'Before people had heard of me it was easier to find engagements,' he exclaimed; 'it's since people know me I can't get shopped.'

'You know what I mean, Galbraith. What can I do? Answering the advertisements in *The Era* is no use – nobody ever answers *me*. It amounts to this, if I don't find something else very soon, I shall have to leave the profession!'

The imminence of such a catastrophe did not seem to thrill Galbraith; he puffed smoke placidly.

'Where were they when you came up?' he asked. 'Is it near my cue?'

'No, Miss Lane hadn't been on yet; you've heaps of time. Do you think I shall ever do any good, Galbraith?'

'You'll do better than you're doing now, boy. I don't think you'll ever play Hamlet.'

'Look here, I couldn't ask many, in the sort of crowds I've been with; but you can tell me, you're a finished actor –'

'Finished and done for,' assented Galbraith cheerfully.

'Not if you'd have enough will! Any management would be glad to have you if they could rely on your resolutions. I don't want to fool myself; tell me the truth. I know I lack experience – and I can't get experience if I don't get parts – but supposing I *can* hold out and I do get the experience, am I ever likely to succeed? Do you think I've any gift for the stage?'

Galbraith had been before the public for thirty years, but Tatham had put a question that no actor had ever asked him before. He reflected before he spoke.

'Laddie,' he said, and he had no aspiration to make epigrams, 'the greatest gifts for the stage are money, and luck. Almost anybody can learn to act fairly well in time; and if you have money, you can pay premiums, and you can take a theatre, and you can commission popular authors to write parts that fit you. In a first-class stock company of the old days, Mr Albert Jernyngham would be playing 'Charles, his friend' – he has money, or, rather, he has people behind him with money, and so he's an actor-manager and plays the impassioned hero. Leaving money out of it, luck's the chief thing – with good luck yon rise, and with bad luck you stick. Good luck gave Fatty Spencer, who has never played any character but himself in his whole career, the chance to make a hit at the old Diadem; they happened to want just such a personality as his in Pulteney's *Lies for a Living*. Fatty's very defects shone as

6

priceless merits. The public shrieked at him, and he's been engaged to play himself in other pieces, at big terms, ever since. Plenty of men who could act him off the stage are feeding at Lockhart's. Tipplers? Improvident? Not a bit of it – just bad luck. They aren't like me, they haven't themselves to blame. Somehow they never chance to get shopped in a thing that runs. They're engaged for West End shows, they give their time to rehearsals, and they get good notices. But the play's a frost, and in a month or six weeks they're out again. Perhaps you suppose they needn't be out for long, if the critics praise them? Optimism of youth, Tatham; there's no continuous service of engagements even for the Fatties. Besides, by and by they get known as Jonahs. That's a reputation that ruined an actor who'd been said by the Press to be the greatest tragedian that England had had since Edmund Kean. In his case, as a matter of fact, it was all bunkum, for he had been in several runs, but he did get called a Jonah, and it settled him. Once let a manager say of a man, or woman, "Oh, yes, very clever, be excellent in the part, of course, but an unlucky name – never seen in a success," and it's likely to mean a vacation of twelve months in the year.'

He knocked the dust from his pipe, and went leisurely downstairs. Tatham, when he had washed, and changed his clothes, returned there too. He did not leave the theatre yet. Most of the players would travel to London in the morning, like himself, but others foresaw mean streets in Liverpool and elsewhere, and there were goodbyes and good wishes to be exchanged. He loitered in the wings and listened to Galbraith fervidly delivering a speech of hackneyed clap-trap which he ridiculed in the dressing rooms. The unsophisticated audience greeted its climax with a burst of applause, while behind the wavering walls of the prodigal's narrow chambers a grubby scene-shifter wheeled forward the porch of the 'Old Home' for the final set. The 'Old Home', to the accompaniment of incidental music, played out of tune by an exiguous orchestra, was duly presented. The faithful housekeeper, who remembered the dear young master when he was a boy, bless his heart, attitudinised at the right of the stage, to hearken jubilantly to a peal of wedding-bells, which the prompter, as usual, sounded at the left; and an anxious leading man, on the verge of unemployment, declaimed as a radiant bridegroom to a despondent leading lady whom he might

7

never meet after tonight, that 'in the golden years before them they would never part again'.

The curtain fell. The company scurried to tear off their costumes and pack their small belongings. Tatham knew that all the men, excepting Galbraith, who had drunk nothing but tea and barley-water for ten days, were impatient to get outside before the bars closed. In their haste to do so, some would neglect to remove their paint. The back of the stage seemed suddenly to have dissolved into the night – the canvas meadows had been hauled into the 'flies', and a real moon displayed confusion in a freezing yard. A vicious wind swept the bare stage as 'The Old Home' and 'The Strong Room in the Bank of England' were stacked on to a wagon.

By twos and threes the company reappeared, carrying garments rolled in newspaper, and non-descript luggage made of straw: 'Well, ta-ta, dear!' 'See you some day!' 'Coming next door, cully?' Among the last to descend was Elsie Lane, a girl whose characterisation of an Irish waif supplied the one touch of humanity that the piece contained. She, too, had found engagements in the West End, but, unlike Galbraith, she had never had important parts nor been able to establish herself there – perhaps because she wasn't tall enough, perhaps because she wasn't pretty enough, certainly not because she wasn't clever enough. She was one of those actresses of whom the critics continue to write, 'A capital character sketch was afforded by Miss So-and-so, who has yet to attain in London the position to which her talents entitle her.' When a country actress is out of work and old, and all hope has been dead in her for many years, sometimes she re-reads that criticism in her poor book of Press cuttings. Elsie Lane's age now was seven or eight and twenty and with her pale, serious face and her quiet manner, she had seemed to Christopher more adapted to a vicarage than to a theatre until he saw her act.

They went through the stage-door together. Her lodging lay in the same direction as his, and he carried her bag for her. The silent roads were slippery, but he couldn't give her his arm, because he had his own portmanteau in the other hand.

'I suppose you haven't settled for anything else?' she asked as they blundered along. 'No.'

'*I* haven't, either. Isn't it horribly cold!' Her shoulders were hunched under her spring jacket. 'I can lend you today's *Era* if you like; there may be something useful in it.'

'Thanks, I've seen it,' he said; 'I've written. I squandered fourpence on stamps this morning. I shan't hear from anybody.'

'One never does.'

'Well, there's no need for *you* to worry – *you're* sure to be all right one day.'

'It looks like it, doesn't it!' She had applied as a 'Strong Character Actress (tall)' and a 'Smart Juvenile Lady (petite)' and as a 'Useful Lady (to complete company)' – practically as everything except a 'Pathetic Child Actress (accustomed to dying)' and a 'Coloured Songstress'. Enjoined by the advertisers to 'State absolutely lowest', she had stated terms that were abject; commanded to forward 'photos and refs', she had sent the most flattering of her photographs, and referred to the most prominent of the managers by whom she was known. Some of the advertisements had added, 'Silence, a polite negative', and despite the variety of her endeavours, and the stamps that she had enclosed for the photographs to be returned, it was the only politeness that she had received.

'Was it always so difficult?' asked Tatham; 'I haven't been in it very long myself, you know.'

'It has always been just as bad in my time; it was easier before there was so much musical comedy, they say – there aren't so many vacancies as there used to be for people who don't sing and dance. Those who pay the piper call the tune, of course; audiences have got to have what they want; but the musical comedy tune is a funeral march to a good many of *us*. I say, I do wish you'd give me that bag back!'

It was bumping against him provokingly, but he said it wasn't. A belated mill-hand clattered by them. After the mill-hand passed, the white, vivid distance was unpeopled. Saying a little more, they trudged through the sleeping town till the girl's doorstep was reached.

'Thanks awfully,' she said, shivering. 'I'm not sure whether I shall go by the early train tomorrow or not – if we don't meet at the station, goodbye.'

'Goodbye.'

'And good luck!'

He put the bag down, and their numbed hands were clasped for a moment.

'Good luck to *you*, Miss Lane,' he said.

Long afterwards – when he had forgotten in what town it had been – he remembered that walk through white, empty streets, and his wishing her 'luck' on a doorstep.

'Goodbye.'

II

The drawing room at Regent's Park looked palatial after the 'bed-sitting rooms' in which he had been living for the last three months, and he was cordially received. Excepting for an explanation that the spare room would shortly be required for one of the married daughters and that an extra bed had been put for him in his cousin Harold's room, instead – an arrangement which, he surmised, must be vastly irksome to his cousin Harold – there was little to remind him that he was in the way. The family questioned him about his doings, and listened smiling to an account of some incidents of the tour. And when his aunt inquired, 'Of course, you've no idea yet what you're going to do next?' her tone was so light that he could nearly persuade himself that her heart didn't sink when he said 'no'.

Then, by way of contributing gossip of interest, Mr Spaulding informed the group that the son of a neighbour had just gone on the stage and exhibited such ability that he had been engaged at ten pounds a week for two years on end. The hop merchant, astute in his own business, 'knew it for a fact, for the boy's father had told him'.

'Wonderful!' he exclaimed admiringly to his nephew; 'isn't it?'

The wonder was, that he had credited the lie, but Tatham couldn't say so; he answered that it was wonderful indeed.

And Harold, who was a dandy, and was always chaffed for the elaborate care that he took of his clothes, had been so good as to huddle them together disastrously, to make space for the guest's. Some guests are never hilariously content.

In ordinary circumstances, next morning, Tatham would have gone to see his mother, but the lady had recently removed to a boarding house at Sweetbay, so he lunched with his aunt. The other men were in the City.

'Sweetbay must be much nicer for her than Dalston,' he said; 'I was very glad to hear she was going. Does she like it, do you know?'

'I think she does,' said Mrs Spaulding; 'yes, I think she likes it very much better. She'd been anxious to get away from London for a long time, she told me.'

'Oh, you've seen her?' He was pleased, for the Spauldings had no great liking for his mother; their invitations to her were few, and their services perfunctory.

'No – er – I did want to ask her to come and stay with us for a week, but we've had such a houseful all the winter that there was really no opportunity – there have been friends of the boys staying here, and one thing and another. I had a letter from her. She said she didn't want to worry *you* about it – you were doing all you could – but she wasn't comfortable where she was, and there was a place at Sweetbay that would take her for very little more.'

'You've sent her money again? That was awfully kind of you.'

'Oh, well, of course, we couldn't let her want – it doesn't amount to a great deal. One would like to do more than that, but –' She sighed. 'Your uncle has so many claims upon him, you've no idea! … Of course it's unfortunate you find the stage such uphill work. If you could get regular engagements it'd be different. You know, I wonder you don't try for a good part at a first-class theatre, Chris. Modesty's all very well, but there's such a thing as being too modest; I think you're a little too – er – I think you're a little too slow to move. I don't think you've enough confidence in yourself. If you never look for better things, you'll never get them, you know; you mustn't expect the prizes of your profession to come and look for *you*.'

'You don't quite grasp the position,' he ventured. 'As an unknown man, I might spend years 'trying for a good part in a first-class theatre' without getting so far as a word with the manager. If I didn't accept the kind of thing that's possible, I should never get anything at all.'

She replied by a reference to an actor who had lately made a successful first appearance in London after twenty years of struggle and privation. 'There's a new young man just 'come out',' she said; 'we saw him the other night and he's excellent. I daresay you could have done it just as well – he looks something like you; he's a beginner, I had never heard his name before. You need to aim higher, Chris, you want more pluck. Of course you've got *us*, and we shall always be very glad to have you here – when we can put you up — but I should like to see you do better for your own sake; I am sure you'd be happier if you were more independent.'

Chicken stuck in his throat.

'If Uncle George can still give me a berth, I'm ready to go into the City tomorrow,' he said thickly.

'Oh, nonsense, there's no occasion to do anything impetuous like that! It really all depends on how long – er – whether your prospects improve or not. Of course, if things go better with you soon, well and good; of course we're quite ready to make ourselves responsible for your mother altogether while you're out of an engagement, just as we've always been. Only you ought to bustle as much as you can and not let the grass grow under your feet, you know! Because if you do have to give up your profession and turn your mind to other things, it'd be a mistake to begin too late. You're not a boy, Chris, and – er – naturally, you'd have a lot to learn before you could hope to be of much use to your uncle,… A little more?'

Nor did he want any cheese. And there was no grass growing under his feet that afternoon on the sloppy pavements of the Strand. He was bound for his agent's. He spoke of Mr Albemarle as his 'agent' because a booking fee had been paid to secure Mr Albemarle's interest. Mr Albemarle did not speak of Tatham as his 'client' because he did not remember Tatham's name. A narrow staircase led to a sparsely furnished apartment, of which a conspicuous feature was a vast assortment of faded photographs. There were photographs of sirens being arch in musical comedies, of heroines being distraught in dramas, of heroes propping brows with forefingers and straining violently to look profound. A goodly number of the originals waited in attitudes of despondence on the forms that lined the walls, and at a table in the corner a young woman with dyed hair, piled over a cheap and obvious frame, was clicking a typewriter.

Tatham discovered space to sit down, and glanced round the room to see if any acquaintance was present. All were strangers to him. From Kennington and Camberwell, from Brixton and East Ham, the theatre folk had journeyed, not a few of them afoot, in the prayer that they might 'hear of something'. They had put on the least shabby of their clothes and to Tatham's eyes the women looked less indigent than the men, but their flowered hats and flimsy smartness shrieked their poverty to one another. Many of the crowd had spent a morning of dejection 'making the round' of the agents' offices. When Mr Albemarle failed them, they would thread their way along the crowded Strand again – with aching feet, and empty stomachs, and affected jauntiness, hoping to the last. They might meet a 'pal who knew of something', or who would, at least, be 'good for a glass of bitter'. There might be a shady manager collecting a new company in the public houses; their salaries with him would be uncertain, but even to take a risk would be better than to go back with no news at all. There were wives and children awaiting the return to Kennington and Camberwell; there were lodging-house keepers clamorous for rent. Today the Strand is wider, but the progress of the players in it just as slow.

It was four o'clock when Tatham was at last admitted to the agent's presence. The gentleman was occupied at a desk. He had a silk hat on his head, and a long cigar in his mouth, each at an angle of forty-five degrees.

'Well, Mr – er,' he said hurriedly, 'I'm afraid I've nothing for you today; things are very quiet just now.'

Never had Tatham heard him say anything more optimistic since the occasion when the fee was paid. But again a forlorn effort to prolong the scene proved useless.

The actor went slowly out. He had not paid a booking fee at any other office; he was not in a position to pay one now. He was not a chorus girl; some chorus girls were able to secure agents' interest without that formality. Blankly he questioned, as he had questioned on the same spot a score of times, what course was open. He felt weak, futile, and contemptible for being so, yet what could he do? He remembered how, despairing one night under the portico of a theatre, where an ex-Society woman was attracting all London by her beauty, he had drooped in the glare gazing at her photographs and thinking she must be compassionate. He remembered how he had pencilled on his card an appeal for a minute's interview and sent it in to her, and how he had shrunk from a scene-shifter's eyes as the fellow brought him her curt refusal. 'What could he do?' At the foot of a career in which, for all but the moneyed and the influential, the potent factor is Chance, he could do nothing but what he did, possessing his soul in patience, and in his uncle's house. And every evening his uncle asked, 'Well, any news?'

So six weeks went by.

'Well, any news?' He meant it kindly, but his guest came to dread the return from the City and that question.

'No, sir.'

'Humph!' The tone conveyed his reflections.

One wet afternoon, when Tatham, having gone down from Mr Albemarle's office, loitered in the shelter of the street door, something happened. Nothing sensational – Mr Albemarle came down too. As the client stood wondering which way to turn next, the agent brushed past him, and loitered also, looking to right and left for a cab.

'Rotten weather!' he said casually to Tatham.

'Filthy, isn't it?' said Tatham. 'Will you come and have a drink?'

Now, in Mr Albemarle the proposal of a drink aroused no such rejoicing as it inspired in many of his humbler clients; he could afford to drink at his own expense, and did so very often, but it happened that at the moment the suggestion fell pleasantly on his ears. All the same, he hesitated. Coming from the lips of an obscure young 'pro', the invitation was either a strange 'bit of luck' or a piece of 'infernal cheek'. He looked Tatham in the face before he spoke.

'I don't mind if I do,' he said graciously.

So lowly is the path to histrionic fame that the Varsity man was conscious of appearing to have improved his position as he entered the Bodega with Mr Albemarle. And, indeed, a dozen loungers there regarded him curiously.

'What'll you have?' he asked.

'Mine's the usual,' said the personage to the barman. He waved a condescending hand in several directions. 'Things are very quiet just now,' he remarked, forgetting that he had just delivered his stock phrase in the office.

'I find it their normal state. You "think you'll be able to find me something next week", do you?'

'What?' Obviously he was surprised, but he recovered himself in an instant. 'Oh, I daresay. Always drop in when you're passing, that's the best way – always pleased to see you. If anything turns up, there you are!'

'I've been dropping in for eighteen months. Nothing has turned up so far. My name's Christopher Tatham.'

'Of course it is,' said Mr Albemarle. 'I know your name very well. I can't shop everybody; there aren't enough parts to go round, Latham, old chap. I'd shop the whole blessed profession, if I could, what do *you* think? – it'd suit *me* all right; but you see what it is, there's too many at the game. What's your line?'

'I've been playing character. "Tatham" not "Latham".'

'I remember now – it had slipped my memory just for the moment.' The barman put the glasses on the counter. 'Here's fortune!'

'But what I want to play is lead.'

'Lead. Right!'

'Do you think you could manage it for me?'

'Do I think I could manage it?' echoed Mr Albemarle. He looked into Tatham's eyes significantly, and his dramatic pause was so protracted that his stare became embarrassing. 'Do I think I could manage it? No, I don't 'think', Latham – I know!'

'That's encouraging.'

'Who made Bernard Leigh?' The query was darted aggressively. 'Who made Eric Latimer? Would Billy Hudson be where he is if it hadn't been for me?' Tatham much feared he had offended him for ever. 'What I can't 'manage' ain't worth managing.'

'I suppose not.'

'Don't worry.' After all, he hadn't been offended – his leer was supremely reassuring. It conveyed a secret compact between himself and Tatham, was charged with esoteric confidences which, though Tatham failed to understand them, promised to flourish master-keys among portals to fame. 'Leading men with the right appearance ain't difficult to shop.'

The next instant, with appalling swiftness, he drained his whisky-and-soda and turned to go. Hope swooned.

'Have another!'

'What? No, no more… well one, for luck!' He imbibed the second leisurely, but discoursed without a break on the abominable ingratitude that he had experienced at the hands of theatrical stars who owned their eminence to his services. Suspensive, Tatham waited for a chance to interpose a question. At last, when the other was saying 'Hell' as a prelude to a farther reminiscence, he exclaimed:

'You know, I'm awfully keen on getting something at once, Mr Albemarle! I've got to find another engagement right off. Of course the money's an object – I depend on the profession – but I'm not standing out for terms. Now, how soon do you think you could get me a leading part, at, say — well, at any figure at all? Frankly! You can't do it this evening, or tomorrow morning, but give me an idea when it might be. That's not asking too much, is it?'

Something in the appeal went home to Mr Albemarle, also the second drink was humanising him. He was temporarily truthful.

'Look here,' he said familiarly, 'you want a shop, don't you? What's the good of kidding about 'leading business'? What you want's a bit every Saturday morning to pay your way, like everybody else; ain't I right?'

'Perfectly right,' said Tatham, dismayed.

'Very well, then! *you* know, and *I* know it's not a scrap of use your opening your mouth too wide and calling yourself a "leading man". Jump at whatever you can get, that's my advice to you. They're sending out a tour from the Sceptre – get round there tomorrow, twelve sharp. Ask for Mr Bailey. Say I sent you. Mind, I can't promise anything'll come of it – you won't be the only one on the spot, but it's a tip. It's a big cast, and they haven't settled for any of the small parts yet.'

The descent from the prospect seen five minutes ago was steep, and the cost of the entertainment alarming – so alarming that Tatham determined to walk to Regent's Park, instead of taking a bus. But as he turned down Bedford Street he was not disconsolate. There was at any rate a chance of sorts.

III

There were eighteen parts to be filled for the provincial tour of the play at the Sceptre Theatre, and actors and actresses desirous of filling them were informed that Mr Bailey was to be found in the business manager's office upstairs. When Tatham, who arrived betimes, explored the quarter indicated, not more than fifty to sixty applicants sat and stood about the landing, awaiting admittance to the room; but their number was continuously reinforced. By half-past one, when Mr Bailey, having disposed of other matters, proceeded to attack the task before him, the staircase had become impassable, and at the foot, groups of men sat morosely on the ground.

Behind the enamelled door, visible only to the most fortunate, the eagerly sought interviews seemed, to those interviewed, unpromisingly brief; to those outside, they seemed eternal, and as the weary hours lagged by, several girls who could find no space to sit, clung weakly to the banisters.

It was Tatham's turn at last.

One girl's limbs felt as if they must give way; she screwed up the courage:

'Oh, do let me go next!'

'I beg your pardon – certainly!'

The promptness of the assent amazed her. She turned and regarded him thankfully as he drew back. In that throng of wearied mediocrities fighting for bread in an overstocked profession, a man and a girl's gaze met for the first time, and they smiled at each other.

So, although he had no idea who she was, Tatham trusted, while he continued to stand there, that behind the enamelled door the interview was proving satisfactory to her. And when she came out, he glanced at her inquiringly. Did she shake her head? he wasn't sure; but she had made her meaning clear. 'I'm sorry,' he murmured as she passed.

The enamelled door opened again and an underling appeared on the threshold. He said in a high-pitched voice, 'Ladies and gentlemen are not to wait, please; Mr Bailey can't see any more!'

Dismay gripped Tatham's heart. Courtesy may cost a theatrical engagement, which is one of the reasons why there is no super-abundance of it in the theatrical world.

A murmur of consternation swelled over the landing; from the landing to the lowest step it travelled, and was echoed in the hall. As the girl started to go down, the packed rows of applicants broke into disorder, and the view on the staircase was a jumble of dejected backs. She lingered an instant for Tatham to be beside her.

'I hope you haven't lost anything by giving me your turn?'

'Oh, I don't suppose so; I daresay all the men's parts were settled before you went in.'

It was possible, however, that none was settled, that Mr Bailey intended to make his selection later among the men who had had the luck to be seen.

'It was awfully kind of you.'

'It was nothing.'

She was very young, perhaps no more than seventeen, but she had been bred in a calling in which few girls remain bashful long. The tone in which she spoke to him was the frank, familiar tone of a young woman at once unacquainted with reserve, and well accustomed to take care of herself; the gaze she raised to him, from a face which had pink-and-white youthfulness for its chief charm, was steadily unembarrassed. When she represented a girl of her own years on the stage, of course, she comported herself with more juvenility than any girl of seventeen that ever lived, for it is a theatrical convention that girls of seventeen caper about a drawing room as if they were seven, but she crossed a room without capering in real life.

He was good looking, and his depression was manifest. She spoke again: 'I'm most awfully grateful to you, really! I felt as if I couldn't stand it another second, or I wouldn't have had the cheek to ask you.'

'It wasn't any use though, eh?'

'I don't think so – he took my name, but I don't fancy it'll come off. Have you been out long?'

'About six weeks.'

'Oh, that's not so bad,' she said; 'I've been doing nothing for months. What were you with last?'

He told her the title of the melodrama in which he had toured last, and wondered if he could add 'Good morning' without being abrupt, for he was in no humour for small-talk with a stranger. But evidently her fatigue was not mental. She continued to question him; and their passage to the street was of necessity slow. On the pavement they came to a standstill together.

'What shall you try for now?' she inquired.

'I've no idea. Have you heard of anything else?'

'No, I must have a look at the ads in today's *Floats*. I haven't seen it yet.'

His distaste for her companionship was passing, even it had already passed. He foresaw that he would feel very lonely in another minute, as he moved aimlessly along; the girl's interest in his prospects was not unwelcome.

'I haven't seen it, either,' he said. 'There's a newsagent's round the corner – let's go and get a copy.'

And then the girl did a happy thing – she exclaimed 'Come on,' and laughed. Precisely at what she laughed she didn't know, but on a sudden his spirits rose, and he liked her.

His spirits dropped when snow began to fall, for the purchase of *Floats* had left him with fivepence for his capital and he could not take her into a confectioner's. They sought employment, studying the advertisement columns together, in the sheltered quietude of a mews. Because he was an impecunious gentleman he was humiliated at having to shelter her there. Because she was a little mummer in the rank and file of 'the profession' she was admiringly surprised by his humiliation.

'I think it was very generous of you to buy the paper,' she said; you might have seen it in a bar and had a drink for the money... What's there funny about it? Go on, now, find something useful, do! – this won't buy the baby a frock.'

'Well, here's something,' he announced. '"Wanted, to rehearse next week, Full Company (with exceptions). To reliable artistes very long tour assured." What do you say to that?'

'It's the best of them yet. Let me look; where's one to write? Oh, "Call"! Where is it? "20 Thackeray Gardens, Clapham Junction.

Three to six." Thackeray was an author, that's where they got that name from. What time is it now?'

He glanced at his watch. 'Nearly five. I say, you must be starving!'

'No, I'm not; I took a sandwich with me – I knew what it'd be. Oh, well, it's no good *my* going to Clapham.'

'Why?'

'I couldn't get there soon enough.'

'It won't take you any longer to get there than it takes me.'

'I haven't enough money in my purse. I should have to go home first and borrow it from mother – it's too far; we're in diggings at Notting Hill.'

They considered ruefully. A brougham swung round the mews, and startled them backwards into a puddle.

'Fivepence won't do it, I suppose?' said Tatham, looking at his boot.

'I don't know; I forget. Anyhow, it'll be a tinpot sort of show. I'm not sure that it's good enough.'

'*Any* show for *me*,' he said. 'I'll tell you what –'

'Well, *you* can go, of course; fivepence'll be enough for one.'

'I'll tell you what: let's hurry up and find a pawnbroker's, and I'll pop my watch.'

'As if I'd let you – just to pay my fare!'

'Well, why shouldn't I?'

'It isn't likely. Popping your watch for me!'

'I should have to pop it for myself tomorrow. Come on, there's a good girl, don't waste time! Look here, if *you* don't go, *I* shan't go, either. That's a fact. I mean it.' He stood looking in her eyes until she smiled. Her smile lit her face very prettily.

'You *are* a nice boy,' she said.

She did indeed think him very nice, and when they had found a pawnshop and she waited for him outside, the pleasing fancy crossed her mind that it was 'almost as if they were married'.

'How much did they lend you on it?' she asked when he came back. A new authority was in her tone.

'Thirty-five shillings.'

'My! It must have been a fine watch.'

21

'Don't speak of it in the past; I hope to see it again,' he said. 'Which is our way — we go from Victoria, don't we? We'd better take a bus from Charing Cross.'

'You haven't told me your name?'

'Christopher Tatham. What's yours?'

'Peggy Harper. I knew a "Chris" once; he was a ventriloquist,' she observed. 'This is my card.'

The card told him no more than the name that she had already communicated; the passion of ladies in the lower ranks of his profession for distributing their printed cards at every opportunity surprised him again after she had paused among the crowd, to rummage in a pocket that took a long time to discover.

The presence of the other passengers did not constrain her on the journey, and he found it agreeable enough – far pleasanter than if he had been alone. It was not unamusing to wander among mean streets, inquiring for Thackeray Gardens with a happy-go-lucky girl who said, 'I daresay we shall have come out here for nothing, after all,' and laughed, as if coming to Clapham for nothing would be a capital joke. It was fun to wait with her in the unprepossessing parlour of a lodging-house and hear her whisper, with a peremptory nod as the doorknob turned, '*You* speak first!'

The advertiser – who, it transpired, called himself Armytage – was evidently attired for the occasion. He wore a frock-coat, in combination with a summer waistcoat, much crumpled, and the trousers of a tweed suit. A garnet pin ornamented the wrong portion of a made-up tie. Early in the interview he confessed, with a lugubrious shake of the head, that long as he had been in management, he had not realised until this afternoon what a multitude of actors and actresses were out of work. The overture sounded unpromising, but it appeared by the light of his later remarks that vacancies might possibly remain in the company for just such 'artistes' as Tatham and Miss Harper. His intention was to open in three weeks' time at Sweetbay, he informed them, and 'the money, though small, was sure'. Figures revealed it to be small indeed. On taking a note of their references and addresses, he was plainly impressed by a terrace in Regent's Park and regarded Tatham with new interest.

'I suppose you could dress the part,' he said – 'got a classy modern wardrobe?'

'I've got clothes, yes,' said Tatham. He hoped with increased force that the part was a good one, since his mother would see him in it.

'"Dress well, on and off," I make it a rule; it pays for actors to look like gentlemen. And what about you, my dear – frocks all right?'

'Oh, I should do you credit!' said the girl flippantly. Tatham envied her professional self-possession.

Mr Armytage repeated that they might hear from him in two or three days, and the 'artistes' left the villa thoughtfully.

'He sounds like a humbug,' said Tatham, 'doesn't he?'

'He doesn't sound up to much,' she assented. 'It'll be a rotten show, of course. Frocks? I'd fake up any old rag and be good enough for his crowd. But the money may be safe with him – you can't go by manner; the bogus people often sound the best. I shan't take it if anything else comes along in the meantime, hut he may be all right. He's one of the old school – never been to school; but I was in panto with a manager who might have been his twin brother, and we got paid every Saturday morning as right as rain. Goodness! a lot of the men who leave you stranded might be Johnnies from Oxford and Cambridge, by their clothes and the way they talk. Education don't make people straight; some of the biggest bounders in the profession used to be swells before they went on the stage. I expect *you'll* change – the profession changes everybody.'

'Thank you,' he said.

'Well, you will! it's sure to spoil you – you won't keep like you are now; you can't!'

'Why not?'

'Because they never do.'

'But why not?'

She reflected. 'Well, if fellows behave like cads anywhere else they get cold-shouldered, you see, and in the profession they don't. I suppose it tempts them to be crooked, when they know they won't be thought any the worse for it. I say, this isn't the way to the station – where are you going?'

'We're going to have something to eat,' said Tatham. 'Do you think it's too soon?'

Her eyes widened at him, almost pathetically, and then she broke into a laugh again; there was a note of hysteria in the laugh this time.

'When I'm a star, I'll find out where you are and get you a swagger engagement!'

'I wonder?'

'Look here!' Her voice was sharp, and she stopped short under a gas lamp. 'I never forget a pal.'

'I was only joking.'

'Well, I wasn't. You've been a brick. I'd do things for *you* if I ever got the chance... But I never shall, not at this business, anyhow!'

'Don't you think you'll ever be a star, then?'

'What, me?'

'Why shouldn't you?'

'I'd give up the stage tomorrow if I'd got anything else to do. I'd never have gone on it if I'd had *my* way. What did *you* take to it for?'

'I love it.'

'You *don't*?'

'Oh, I do – really!'

'Well, I am astonished,' she said. 'I should have thought you were ever so much too clever for that. Whatever do you love about it? I think it's a rotten business.'

'It's a rotten business as one is now, but if one gets on, it may be a great art.'

The word 'art' evidently conveyed little to her mind; her voice was puzzled. '*I* don't see anything in it. Of course, I'd like big money, but I'd much rather get it without having to act. I think acting's silly. I don't see how you can be expected to laugh, and cry, and carry on in a part, just as if it was all real.'

'You have to feel as if it were all real while you're studying the lines – you have to ask yourself just how you would say it all if it were something happening in your own life.'

'Oh, my word!' she exclaimed protestingly. Her attention wandered. 'The shops about here don't come up to the West End ones, do they? They're much better than this about Notting Hill.'

They had dinner in a shabby little Italian place – half restaurant, half cake-shop – where they were the only customers. Soup and a fillet, both very indifferent, with stale chocolate eclairs to follow, seemed to her epicurean, and she pronounced the fried potatoes 'a long way better than what you got with pen'orths of fried fish'. The gratification of her appetite, even more, the novelty of being entertained, exhilarated her exceedingly, and she had felt a pleasurable sense of unfamiliar dignity in seeing a bottle of beer opened for her by a shuffling waiter.

It was past eight when Tatham wished her goodnight, after lending her the coppers to take her home. The lateness of his return to Regent's Park had raised expectations, and he was greeted with a chorus of 'Well?' A detailed account of the day's doings, he thought, was likely to be ill received, and he dwelt much more upon his interview at Clapham than upon his disappointment at the Sceptre. He could not, however, avoid creating the impression that he had presented himself at the theatre tardily, and more than ever he was conscious that patience with his career was moribund. This time next month, would he be an actor or a clerk? Instinct proclaimed that his fate was in the unwashed hands of Mr Armytage.

IV

One of the drawing-room windows permitted the anxious to view an exasperating postman for nearly five minutes before he reached No. 12. During the next four days Tatham spent much of his time at that window. In a letter to his mother he had mentioned that there was a prospect of his going to Sweetbay, and the widow had already replied, 'supposing that by now the engagement was settled'. Experience had supplied no grounds for her supposition, but her optimism – or the carelessness with which she had read his letter – would make it additionally distasteful to him to have to say he could not go. And the postman had a letter for every house in the terrace excepting No. 12.

Then, when Tatham wasn't watching, and hadn't heard any knock at the street door, the parlourmaid unconcernedly handed a bulky envelope to him. A part was inside – he was engaged! He had never seen the play; had no idea whether the part was good – was for the present too much excited to do more than whip over the pages to ascertain whether it was long or short; but thanksgiving throbbed in him – he was engaged!

'It's come!' he announced rapturously to his aunt. And today he looked forward to his Uncle George's return from the City and the question, 'Any news?'

Was Miss Peggy Harper engaged too? he wondered.

In an unfurnished room over a public house, where the rehearsals were conducted, it became evident to him that she was not. Among the dreary-faced women and disreputable-looking men who mumbled and moved about the room under Mr Armytage's direction, no Miss Harper appeared. Tatham regretted her absence, for in the environment in which he found himself the arrival of almost any acquaintance would have been welcome. With a single exception, he saw that the 'artistes' around him represented the lowest grade of the theatrical world, and there recurred to him distressingly that sense of shame which had been one of his earliest experiences in his profession.

The exception referred to was a smartly dressed youth of about nineteen, who, by his clothes and unfamiliarity with stage 'business', excited many humorous winks among the other men. He was, plainly, embarrassed and unhappy, and since the premium demanded of him had been paid and the cheque swiftly cashed, the manager was at no pains to afford encouragement.

'Now then, you!' he bawled, 'don't you know there's supposed to be a window there? Are you going to walk through a third-floor window at night? We want actors, not acrobats. Hi, Lonsdale!' The youth, with the co-operation of his sisters, had selected the name of 'Vernon Lonsdale'. He had grown his hair long, and they had pictured him in romantic situations, looking like Kyrle Bellew. Just now he looked like sacrificing his premium.

'I beg your pardon,' he stammered; 'I didn't know where the window was meant to be.' He hurriedly advanced, and stood, with pale cheeks, awaiting his next cue.

A melancholy female read indistinctly from her part some lines that concluded with the word 'menace'. She pronounced it to rhyme with 'grimace', and the youth, not recognising her intention, remained mute.

'Go on, my boy,' roared Armytage; 'why the hell don't you go on?'

'I haven't had my cue,' said the youth resentfully.

'Show me your part,' commanded Armytage. 'There you are, it's in your part right enough – "men*ace*"!'

'Oh, "*men*ace"?' said the youth.

'What's that – what d'ye call it, my boy? "*Men*ace"? Rats! That's extant, that's altogether extant.' He evidently relished his discovery of "extant" which he seemed to believe was a scholarly synonym for 'out of date'. He looked round for Tatham. 'Isn't "*men*ace" extant, eh?' he inquired.

'Quite,' said Tatham. His gaze met the discomfited youth's with a twinkle.

'Of course it is,' said the manager. 'And even if it wasn't, "men*ace*" is more dramatic. Go on, young feller, my lad, we can't spend the day here teaching you the ABC, you know!'

Tatham, recognising the school into which he had fallen, sat resolved to declaim his lines in the most melodramatic fashion of which he was capable when his turn came; but, even so, he was not at the outset unnatural enough. Intense dejection weighed upon him as he laid intelligence upon the altar of expediency. The art of acting itself tottered on the pedestal of his enthusiasm, and miserably he questioned whether his dignity was any higher than a performer's who stuffed flaming tow into his mouth in a road.

Pity for young Lonsdale depressed him, too, as from day to day he beheld the youth jeered at and bullied. He was not a brilliant youth; it was difficult to credit him with enough capacity to make his way in any walk of life; but his numerous suits of clothes suggested that he might have squandered as much as fifty pounds to secure a professional debut on the stage, and the sum at least entitled him to civility.

'It's very different to what I thought it was going to be,' he complained to Tatham, in a girlish voice; 'he was awfully polite when I saw him at Clapham. And he said it was a good part. *I* don't call it a good part, do you? There's only that little pathetic bit in the third act that I take any interest in.'

'There isn't a good part in the piece,' answered Tatham.

'Oh, don't you think so? I think some of them are all right. Only the people are so common; they're an awfully low lot, aren't they? No, I don't call it at all a good part now, excepting for that little pathetic bit in the third act. It looked all right when I read it at home, but it seems so different at rehearsal – I'm always being bundled about; when I do come to a speech, somebody cuts in before I've got the last word out. Don't you know what I mean?'

'Yes, I know very well. He cuts in to prevent you getting any applause. That's the reason for that.'

'Oh, I say! I say, but that's awfully mean, isn't it? I didn't think actors did that sort of thing. I wonder it's allowed.'

'It *isn't* allowed by people who're in a position to stand up for their rights. Beginners have got to grin and bear it, if the manager doesn't interfere.'

'Oh, I shouldn't like to complain! They'd be so rude, wouldn't they?'

'Yes, they'd be very rude,' said Tatham. 'I'm not complaining, either – what does it matter, anyhow, in a thing like this? The person who hasn't shaved for a week is going to spoil my best scene for me; he thinks I don't know enough to understand that he's trying to spoil it, but I do.'

'I never hear him cut *you* short,' said Lonsdale enviously.

'No, he can't break in very often, but he keeps getting further behind me at every rehearsal – in the theatre I shall have to turn my back to the audience all the time I talk to him, and that'll make him look the chief figure in the scene, although he isn't meant to be.'

'Will it, really? Why should it? He must be an awfully vain brute, mustn't he? Well, one thing!' he laughed gleefully; 'that beast of a comedian can't try the same dodge on *me*, with my little pathetic bit in the third act, for he's got to be sitting down, writing a letter, while I say it.'

The journey to Sweetbay was made on a Sunday morning; the heterogeneous garments that they donned for travelling gave to the company an appearance even more repellent than they presented in the public house. The train reached the prim little watering-place at the hour when many of the residents passed the station on their return from church; and as the players, burdened with strange hand-luggage, straggled into their midst, Tatham heard young Lonsdale panting behind him.

'I *say*!' exclaimed the boy – his face was aghast – 'this is awful, isn't it? Why on earth don't they have any cabs here?'

Tatham was execrating it, too. 'I suppose nobody arrives in the place on Sunday, excepting us. But I can't afford cabs, myself. Where are you going to stay? have you arranged anywhere?'

Like Tatham, the tyro had still to discover apartments, and it appeared that he meant to seek them on the Parade. Tatham reflected. It did not concern him, but the lad seemed pathetic in his ignorance.

'Look here,' he said, 'I don't want to meddle, but I'm afraid you'll find it very expensive if you hang out in first-class diggings on a tour like this. I don't mean just the rent; I'm afraid you'll find it comes very dear in other ways – you'll be a "mark" for all the men in the crowd to borrow money from. I expect they'll be cadging from you anyhow – "prossing" they call it – but if they hear of your lolling on balconies on Parades, you'll be preyed upon frightfully, they'll ask you for half-sovereigns.'

'I say!' said Lonsdale. He put two and two together. 'You think they guess it's my first engagement?'

'Yes, I think they divine it,' said Tatham. 'If you take my advice, you'll stay in the same sort of lodgings as everybody else. You needn't have a bedroom and parlour combined, of course, but I should keep to the professional addresses, if I were you.'

'Thanks,' said the boy. 'I'm much obliged to you; it's awfully decent of you to give me the tip.' He sighed. 'It *is* different to what I thought it'd be. And the *girls*! I always thought actresses were pretty – why, I never saw such a crew in my life!'

At this moment, among the returning congregation, an elderly lady approached, in her Sunday costume, her eyebrows protesting against the troop of vulgar travellers that profaned the pavements. Tatham saw, confused, that the lady was his mother. She recognised her son almost at the same instant, and with pretended pleasure, which ill concealed dismay, stopped short to welcome him.

'Why, Chris?' she faltered. Lonsdale proceeded alone, in the wake of the heavy man and the low comedian, and her perturbed glance followed them. 'Do those people belong to your company?'

'The young one's right enough,' declared Tatham, momentarily vain of Lonsdale. 'Well, how are you, mother?'

'Oh, I'm first-rate. Couldn't you have left your portmanteau at the station? One never sees anybody carrying luggage about on Sunday in Sweetbay.'

'Well, you see, a lot of the things that are in it I shall want tonight. Of course, the arrival isn't pleasant; it never is. We don't always get in at church time, though, thank goodness! Well, tell me, is the boarding house still all right? I was coming to see you this afternoon.'

'Yes, do! Oh yes, there are one or two very smart people there. Let's move round the corner, Chris, we look so bad standing here! Yes, we've quite nice people – an army man and his wife, you'll see them when you come. We play bridge in the evening. Don't say what you're doing here – I shouldn't like them to know you're on the stage. I lost fourteen-and-sixpence the other week. Nearly "broke" me!' She tittered, as at an incident of a humorous nature. 'Had to write to the Spauldings.' A titter announced this to be funnier still. 'Said I wanted new boots. They sent me a sovereign – I was saved!' The mirthfulness of the recital overwhelmed her.

He perceived, with mixed emotions, that her removal had invigorated his mother, mentally at least. The humiliated pensioner that he remembered in Dalston had become accustomed to dependence, and even callous to it.

'Perhaps somebody'll see my name on the playbills,' he warned her.

'Oh, I don't think so; we don't take much notice of the theatre here; only rubbish comes down. Anyhow, I shan't say anything about it unless they ask me. Well, I mustn't wait! we have luncheon at one o'clock – we have luncheon on Sundays, too; we dine late on Sundays, just the same as any other day there! It's not at all like an ordinary boarding house; they don't take everybody, Mrs Harrington's very particular who she takes. Then you'll be round about half-past four? Make yourself look as nice as you can. Put on the best suit you've got, Chris. I hope none of them'll see you carrying your portmanteau. Wasn't there a cab in the yard? I wonder you don't jump into a cab for a shilling.'

A shilling! It had often been a strain on his finances to buy a penny postage stamp for the letter that contained his remittance to her.

He continued his way thoughtfully. The current issue of *Floats*, seen in London, had informed him in which streets the few theatrical apartment-houses of Sweetbay were situated, and when he had found a 'combined room', he was provided with a cut from the landlady's joint. Well, after what his mother had said, it was to be presumed that she would not go to see his performance. He would be much relieved if she didn't, yet he was hurt that she did not wish to do so. As he smoked a pipe he was conscious that the eagerness with which he had anticipated his visit to her had subsided; and, when at half-past four he paid it, he found himself increasingly dull.

It served, however, to confirm his conjecture that the lady's presence at the theatre was not to be feared; she explained that a matinée always gave her a headache, and that 'of course, she couldn't sit in a theatre alone at night.' Besides, her going would 'be sure to cause a lot of talk about the piece, and somebody might have the curiosity to look at the cast.' She thought it was 'much safer for her to keep away'.

'Oh, and, Chris,' she said, before the alleged army man and his nondescript wife appeared, to make painful persiflage over pale tea, 'don't say you're stopping here, say you're going back to town this evening! See? If Mrs Harrington heard you were here for a week, she'd want to know where you were staying, and I shouldn't like her to know you were doing it on the cheap.'

He was struggling for advancement on a squalid plane of an unpromising vocation, and perhaps was a fool to have chosen it; but very often he had struggled unfed that his mother might receive the expected pound intact, and he winced to know she was ashamed of him.

Next night he was ashamed of himself; he rejoiced that she had not come to witness his ignominy among these barn-stormers. Again, they made him marvel. They blasphemed, in the wings, at the coldness of the public, they cursed the limitations of the stage, they anathematised the blunders of the limelight man; but that they were figuring in a preposterous play, in a manner that was devoid of talent, or intelligence, or a single virtue, they were blankly and complacently unaware.

Only young Lonsdale had adverse criticism to utter upon a performance; Tatham was alone with him for a few minutes when the other men had hurried to the bars. 'I say,' wailed the debutant – tears stood in his eyes – 'my little pathetic bit in the third act! I don't see how I'm ever going to make a name like this. That beast of a low comedian – he drank out of the inkpot instead of the glass, he carried on like a clown while I was speaking! That little pathetic bit of mine in the third act was the only time the audience laughed.'

But when Saturday came, after five unprofitable nights, the greenhorn of the company was the member least disturbed. Grouped on the stage of the Theatre Royal, Sweetbay, the barn-stormers waited for Mr Armytage to appear with their salaries. The gentleman was due at noon. At a quarter to one they stood waiting still, and comments had ceased. When the hour struck, the faces of the crowd were blanched; everybody looked much older.

Upon the matinée announced to commence at 2.30, the curtain did not rise. Few local play-goers were disappointed. Then it was common knowledge that Mr Armytage had been observed departing from Sweetbay by a very early train, among the milk-churns. When he advertised for his next band of victims, his name would not be 'Armytage'.

Yes, the greenhorn was the member of the company least disturbed, for though he had lost his premium, he had lost his eagerness – at any rate, to be associated with a troupe like this one; and he, alone among the 'artistes', was unharassed by the problem of ways and means.

Tatham was stunned by it. From his mother, who had visited him surreptitiously, perturbed lest Mrs Harrington and the army man should 'ever wonder what she was doing down this end of the town', assistance was impossible. His only course was to beg a loan of Lonsdale or to write to the Spauldings. The remembrance of his warning to Lonsdale, as much as the doubt how the sum would be repayable, nerved him to appeal to his aunt.

He lacked the amount of his bill and his fare to London – and a postal order duly reached him. But when he had slunk back to No. 12, where the extra bed had been restored to his cousin Harold's room, Uncle George's proclamation on the hearthrug, after dinner, caused him no astonishment.

'You must see for yourself that this won't work, my boy,' said Spaulding definitely; 'you'll have to give the stage up. You must try to take an interest in something else – you'll have to be satisfied with a berth. I'll do what I can for you, and you'll be able to manage better if you and your mother go into lodgings together; there's no reason for her to remain at Sweetbay. You can take three rooms together somewhere in a cheap neighbourhood, and you'll both of you be much more comfortable that way. You'd better come into the City with me tomorrow morning.'

V

When the dull confusion had cleared from his mind, when the place where he sat had begun to be a familiar place, and he knew, without raising his eyes, that five letter-files fell awry to the left of the mantel-piece, and just what section of a wall and a water-pipe was visible across the glossy red backs of the three bulky account-books that flanked the copying-press, Tatham was surprised to perceive that the intimidating clerks under the green shades around him were becoming no less human than actors. Like the actors that he had deserted, they performed their duties without zest and without expectation. The dream in which some of them had once indulged of being summoned to the chief's presence to receive compliments and a prominent position already looked as fantastic to their minds as the dream of playing Hamlet before Royalty looked to the disillusioned actor evading his washerwoman in Bacup. Just as all the interests of the actors had lain outside the theatre, so all the interests of the clerks lay outside the office. Admitting him by degrees to confidences – somewhat tardily, because he was the 'boss's nephew' – the erstwhile intimidating business men talked of music halls. Eventually they were more confidential than he, for when their conversation turned upon the play, he did not – since it would have rendered the sense of failure still more poignant to him – acknowledge that he had been on the stage. He listened to their criticisms pensively, and accepted their mistakes without remonstrance. Not even the strange assertions of the accountant, a confirmed playgoer, who by reason of his age erred dogmatically, provoked him to correction.

The proposal that she should return to London had not appealed to Mrs Tatham. She had been forced to submit herself to second-class London lodgings during the last two or three years of her husband's life, and she shrank from renewing the experience. Her reply that ill health made the plan very undesirable, of course disposed of the suggestion. Her son was installed in a top bedroom in Doughty Street, and lived alone on the half of a larger salary than his clerical capacities would have gained for him from any stranger. By dint of an indefatigable quest for the cheapest City chop-houses and an avoidance of pudding, he sometimes had a half-crown remaining for the pit of a theatre on

Saturday night. Not often. But there were galleries at a shilling. And his most frequent weakness cost him, in cash, nothing at all. He went in the evening to walk in the Strand.

Formerly he had loathed the Strand; had paced it despairingly and felt that never, so long as he lived, would he be able even to drive through it without resentment. Yet now the street of memories was not without a tender grace, not without a sentimental appeal. Once or twice, craving to see it again in its most intimate aspect, he lunched rapidly on a sandwich and contrived a breathless visit to the Strand during the luncheon hour. Luck was against him. Though he saw many actors, he saw none whom he knew. But it was an emotional promenade, notwithstanding, that saunter from the Gaiety, where he jumped off the bus, to Charing Cross post office, where he turned back wide-eyed. He re-entered clerkdom guiltily – a man with a secret, a clerk who led a double life. When six months had worn away, his gloom held but a single gleam of comfort – the reflection that, distasteful as he found the work, he had never scamped it, never reached his place late nor left it too soon – the comfort of reflecting that his uncle must report upon him warmly. Recognising the salary to be generous, though inadequate, he was proud to have deserved the satisfaction. What his uncle actually reported was that 'Christopher did just what he was set to do, but had no initiative, and would never be worth more than he was getting.'

Nearly a year had passed when Tatham at last happened to meet someone associated with the 'dear dead days beyond recall' and then it was not in the Strand, and it was not anyone whom he had known well. On a Saturday afternoon, in Long Acre, he saw Miss Peggy Harper approaching.

'Hallo, hallo, hallo!' she said, stopping to greet him. For the moment she couldn't recall his name, but she put out her hand genially enough, and they stood smiling at each other.

'How d'ye do?' said Tatham constrainedly. To speak to a girl was such an unusual experience now that he felt shy.

'And what have you been doing with yourself?'

'Oh, I'm all right,' he said. 'You know that tour came to grief? One week, and nobody got his money.'

'What tour?' she said vaguely. 'Oh, oh yes, I remember! Well, what's the best news? Are you doing anything?'

'I – I've given it up. I'm not on the stage any more.'

'Aren't you? Well, good judge too! You can't tell me of anything, then? I thought perhaps you might have told me of a nice vacancy.' She laughed.

'I wish I could. Have you been out of an engagement long?'

'No; I'm only just back from tour. I'm all on my own now. Mother's playing in Australia. I'm in diggings with another girl. I say! have you seen *Ada's No Chicken*?'

He shook his head. 'I don't go to the theatre very often. I can't get seats for nothing now I've left the profession.'

'What rot! Who's to know you've left it? you could write and enclose one of your old cards.'

'Oh, I can't do that,' he said.

'Well, I've got a couple of stalls in my pocket for the matinée this afternoon. The girl I'm living with has got an appointment and can't go with me. If you've nothing to do, you might come.'

'Oh, thanks; I'd like it immensely,' said Tatham. 'What time does it begin?'

'I'm going there now. Come along, then, or we shall be late.'

He wished he had put on his other coat; but it was delightful, nevertheless, to sit in a stall again and talk to an actress. Almost he forgot in moments that he was today a clerk. And although a sixpenny programme and the tea when they came out were items of importance, a florin wasn't much as the price of a trip to another planet.

She gave him her address before they parted, and with alacrity he accepted her invitation to 'come in and see them one of these days'. All the week he found himself looking forward to the visit. The fear that on Saturday she was likely to be at another matinée determined him to wait till Sunday, and he rose on Sunday with an eagerness ludicrously disproportionate to the occasion. A new zest was in his mood, a new interest coloured his outlook – a zest and an interest which the girl would have been incapable of inspiring in him twelve months before, when the realm that she represented had been his own realm too.

She was lodging over a little shop that described itself as 'Dairy and Refreshment Rooms' in Great Queen Street. The shutters were up this afternoon, and he saw no private door; but after he had rung twice, the shop door was opened and he was instructed to 'Come through, please.'

'Second floor,' said the woman. 'Will you go up.'

A glimpse he had of milk-cans, and of stale cakes under glass covers. He mounted a narrow staircase, to knock timidly.

'Come in! Oh, it's you!'

Pleasure was in her voice. The tiny room was lit only by firelight. When she had exclaimed that she was 'jolly glad he had remembered, and that he was to take his overcoat off and put it down anywhere,' he sat by the fire, opposite her, and thought how much cosier it was than his top bedroom.

'Naomi will be down in a minute,' she said; 'she's changing her frock. As soon as she comes you shall have some tea.'

'Is "Naomi" the girl you're living with!'

'Yes, of course it is; did you think it was a servant? Naomi Knight. She talks like you – you ought to get on.'

'Talks like me?'

'I mean she's awfully serious about it all.'

'Oh, as I used to talk?'

'Oh yes, of course – I forgot you weren't in the profession now. What are you doing, then?'

'I told you. I'm in the City.'

'Did you? I don't remember,' she said. 'Do you mean you're in a clerkship? I say! It must be rather a change, isn't it?'

Actually he was conscious that the moment would be beautiful if she were indeed interested to hear what a change it was – if he could make confidences to an actress in the firelight and find her sympathetic. But Peggy Harper chattered on before he could make any answer at all. 'What do you think of our rooms? Rotten, aren't they? But we're so close to everything – look at the time it saves. Where are *you* living?' Again she omitted to wait for his reply. 'When mother settled the Australian engagement, I made up my mind to live near the Strand. No more suburbs for *me*; I'd rather have the pokiest little place about here

37

than the best diggings in Notting Hill or Brixton that ever were – half your day's spent in going backwards and forwards. And look at the fares, how they mount up! I think this is a jolly good pitch. Of course, our food wants watching, but so it does wherever you go. Does your landlady take your things? Everybody says the professional landladies steal less than the others. Have *you* found that? Does *your* landlady let to the profession? I say, it's a funny thing, if anyone steals at ha'porth of bread from a shop once in her life because she's starving she gets sent to prison, but nearly every landlady steals bread and meat and groceries all the year round as a matter of course and you mustn't even complain of it openly, or she blackguards you, besides.'

It was something of a disappointment to find that Miss Naomi Knight was neither very young nor very good-looking. She was revealed as a thin, dark woman who seemed at first to possess no other attraction than a pleasant voice. It was not until he had helped to take the cups and saucers from the cupboard and to clear a good deal of litter from the only table that she uttered anything but trivialities. Then, of course, the talk reverted from the teapot to the stage, and she told him what character she had played last and what she thought of it. He found her ideas on the subject – for he knew the piece – very interesting.

'I said you two'd get on,' cried Peggy. 'I shock her frightfully. I don't know how she puts up with me.'

'Don't be so silly,' said Miss Knight. 'She won't work, Mr Tatham, that's what's the matter with this girl.'

'I'm not going to give myself the hump over Shakespeare, and Ibsen, and things like that. What's the good? I shall never play 'em! Besides, I don't understand what they mean.'

Miss Knight smiled indulgently. 'Some women who do play them don't read them,' she said, 'I was in a company with a woman once who told me she had played in three Shakespearean seasons and never read one of the plays in her life – she had only read her own lines.'

'Do you believe it?' asked Tatham.

'Yes,' she said, 'I quite believe it; I'm sure it was true. The most extraordinary people go on the stage. They haven't any gift for it, and they aren't even earnest about it. I can't make out how they expect to do any good.'

'Hark at her rubbing it into me!' laughed Peggy.

'I wasn't thinking about you at all; you're only a child yet.'

'Child yourself! I shall get up and smack you if you aren't careful. Child, indeed!' She appealed gaily to Tatham. 'Don't you think I'm grown up?'

'I think you're very nice,' he said diffidently.

'There you are? So I am. So are you! I say, do you know this boy lost a shop through me a hundred years ago? That was how we met. "Do let me go in next!" I said. Like that – the pathetic heroine. "With pleasure," he said. Talk about manners, he was a regular Lord Burleigh.'

'Chesterfield's the gentleman you're thinking of, ducky.'

'Oh, well, what's the odds, it's all the same. And then he popped his watch for me. I say, did you ever get it out? Let's see if you've got your watch on!'

He had got it on at last, but he turned very red, and Miss Knight interposed hastily:

'Don't take any notice of her; she wants a good shaking. Where were you both – in London? Are you playing anywhere now?'

'I've given it up,' he said again, 'I'm not an actor.'

'Oh, really? Didn't you care for it?'

'Yes, very much.'

'But that's awfully hard lines on you.' She was attentive, grieved; her attitude invited him to say more.

'It was rather a facer. I'm in a clerkship – I had to do something, and engagements were too difficult to find.'

'But that's cruel!'

'Isn't it beastly rough on him?' exclaimed Peggy brightly, who hadn't thought so till she was told. 'And I'm sure he was clever. Weren't you?'

'I wasn't clever enough to get on.'

'Oh, but you're so young!' said Miss Knight. I think it's dreadfully hard lines on you; I do really. And do you have to go to the City every day?' She seemed to hope that he had found a clerkship in which he was needed only once a week.

'Saturday's a half-holiday; Sunday's a red-letter day – this Sunday. I haven't even come across anyone in the profession till I met Miss Harper.'

'I do think this poor boy's to be pitied,' declared Peggy. Her sympathy, though late, was pleasant. 'Don't you think it's very brave of him, Naomi?' She went a step too far and made him feel ridiculous.

'Won't you tell me more about yourself, Miss Knight? What are you reading now?'

She was reading a novel, and a good one – sufficiently good for him to be surprised to learn that she had heard of it. She talked of it very intelligently. It was easy to see that the study of character fascinated her – her interest in it was not a pose – and Tatham began to feel that although she had made no position in the theatre yet, he was listening to a woman who was destined to be heard of by-and-by. Excepting Elsie Lane, he had known no other actress who impressed him with this conviction, and he could not help reflecting that Peggy Harper was right in saying that they were very dissimilar companions.

Yet, because Peggy was young, and might in moments be called pretty, it was Peggy who lent enchantment to the parlour over the dairy and refreshment rooms on Sundays now. If Miss Knight sometimes said things that came back to him when he had gone, it was Peggy who drew his gaze oftener when he was there. And her chatter had a charm for him too, for was it not always professional! Indeed, it took him much nearer to the wings than Miss Knight's analyses of Shakespeare's heroines. The chance of getting 'shopped' in some obscure company, Naomi's prospect of settling for a part, through Albemarle, the disappointments met with – these topics exercised a fascination over a young man, who, stage-struck from his boyhood, had been compelled to relinquish the stage. Even the slang that she used made the past glow again. If she had been a dressmaker's assistant, or a waitress, her interest would have been slight, but the theatre transmuted her. To him she represented the theatre. He hated the City, and she was the ray of limelight in his life.

'Don't you think he's mashed on you, Peggy?' said Miss Knight one day when they sat talking about him.

'What rot!' said Peggy, with a conscious smile.

'You hum! You know very well he is.'

'Well, what of it anyhow?'

'Oh, nothing!'

And that was the girl's view too. He was 'mashed on her'. It meant to her simply the gratification of having made a conquest. Whether he would tell her that he was 'mashed' even whether she liked him enough to wish him to do so, were matters to which she gave no thought. Why should she, why 'worry to think' since he was too hard up to marry for ever so long? Sufficient for the day was the admiration thereof – and it was the first time that she had found an admirer who was a gentleman.

That he was a gentleman was as forcefully Tatham's attraction to the girl as the fact of her being an actress was her attraction to him. Just as the man knew, when he was willing to remember it, that she was vapid and vulgar, so the girl knew at the back of her little hen's brain that his conversation was much less congenial to her than the banter of the young men with whom she was accustomed to joke. But he was a gentleman! She had no doubt on the point – she had not needed Naomi's confirmation; unerringly she could distinguish, as girls on even a lower social stratum can unerringly distinguish, between gentlemen and the gentlemanly, and to have captivated him flattered her much. It flattered her so much that, even if he had attempted to improve her mind, she would have cheerfully submitted for a time.

Soon his visits were not limited to Sundays; often he sat by the fire in Great Queen Street on Saturdays too. *The Era* was published on Saturday, and if he took in a copy of a paper that she could not afford to buy she was frankly and joyously appreciative. It wasn't, 'Thanks, that's very kind of you, I haven't seen it yet;' it was, 'You *are* a brick! I say, it *is* good of you! *we* can't run to sixpenny papers.' She pretended to surplus silver no more than to histrionic enthusiasm – from motives of self-aggrandisement she pretended nothing, she was spontaneity personified. She was spontaneity personified one Saturday when he arrived to be greeted with the news that her friend had just found an engagement.

'Here, you're just in time; come and congratulate her!' she cried. 'This girl has struck it rich. She has! She's going to play "Mrs Jocelyn" in *Mabel, Go and Put On Your Hat.*'

'Oh, I'm awfully glad!' exclaimed Tatham, for it was an excellent part in a very successful West End comedy by a brilliant writer.

'Isn't it jolly?' said Miss Knight. 'I'm ever so pleased about it; it was only decided this morning. And I shan't have to give up these rooms at the start – that's another good thing, for it's for an eight weeks' tour of the suburbs.'

'And afterwards?'

'Afterwards we go into the provinces, perhaps. That isn't sure yet.'

'You'll be left here alone if she goes away?' he said, turning to Peggy.

'Oh, I don't know what I shall do if she goes away – I couldn't manage to keep on all this by myself; I'd have to put up with a combined room if I was still in town. But there's lots of time to worry about that, I may be in the provinces too before then. I say, I do think it's ripping, her getting such a swagger part!' She was as genuinely elated as if she herself had been fortunate.

'I hope you *don't* go into the provinces too,' he said. 'What'd become of *me*? It's very selfish of you to think of such a thing – the least you can do is to stand out for a London engagement!'

'Yes, likely! What price mother? You'd better drop her a postcard, tell her she's to go on sending me money every week till I'm offered leading business up West. I see mother's face! How many changes have you got, Naomi? have you got to find your own frocks?'

'Yes; but I've got all I want, except the black – I can make my evening frock pass for clean if I cover it up with chiffon. You've seen the piece, Mr Tatham, haven't you? What did you think of the way Miss Stevens played the scene in the third act? Do you remember?'

'I thought she was very good. Didn't you?'

'Y-e-s, I thought she might have done rather more. I didn't think she brought out quite all there was in it; she didn't seem to me to go quite deep enough.'

'I suppose you'll have to copy her?' he asked. 'It must be rather rough, the way all the people have to copy the performances of the London company, whether they want to or not?'

'*I* shan't – not altogether. I may have to do it at the rehearsals, but I shall give my own reading of the part at night.'

'Hear, hear!' said Peggy. 'Don't you be sat on, old girl! I say, this wants celebrating. Hold on a minute, both of you! I shan't pay, I shall tell her to stick it on the bill.' She darted out of the room, and reappeared two minutes later with bottles from the shop. 'It's teetotal – I can't help that, she hasn't got a licence!' she announced to Tatham.

'You'll find tumblers in the cupboard – don't upset the cruet, it's rocky.'

'There are only two there,' said Naomi Knight; 'I took up the other for our teeth.'

'Bring me a cup, then!'

'No, *I'll* have the cup,' said Tatham.

'Give it to *me*!' She struggled with him sincerely, and was victorious. 'Here's to Naomi!'

'Miss Naomi Knight!'

'Here's to everybody!' laughed she.

And then, the importance of the part again, the name of the suburb they were to 'open' in, the absorbing question of the 'chiffon', whether, after all, chiffon would conceal the shabbiness so well as lace. When he sat in the top bedroom that evening, in an armchair with a broken spring, blowing smoke musingly, Tatham wondered how the bohemian scene would look on the stage if a playwright reproduced it there, wondered if there would be any atmosphere in it behind the footlights – two girls, and a young man, all more or less penniless, drinking toasts to the future in ginger ale 'stuck upon the bill'. A comedy, of course, and the younger hostess, Peggy, would be the heroine. The young man, presumably, would be the hero – one would have to make him something more interesting than a clerk at a hop merchant's. A rich man's son, estranged from his family and forgiven later? Nothing very original about that. Still the hero must marry her at the end – he would have to get the money somehow! Earn it? Y-e-s. What at?

Frowning, smiling, with no definite purpose, he pondered the fancy that had come to him – began to discern the dim outline of a plot in it; became all at once unpractical and was a popular dramatist, dizzy with triumph; dropped from Olympus, with a bump, on to the incipient plot and found that it wouldn't do at all. He abandoned the matter. Ridiculous daydream! He resolved to think of something else – and discovered that the comedy was insistent. He jumped up and thrust a chair to the rickety table, and slowly, laboriously proceeded to examine his fancy with pen and ink.

So he took his first step to authorship.

VI

Not the next incident in his acquaintance with Peggy Harper, but the next incident that always remained in his memory, was his travelling beside her in a tram, full of dripping umbrellas, and sitting beside her in a suburban dress circle. Naomi Knight had obtained a pass for them.

He had anticipated the evening with considerable eagerness. At every visit that he had paid during three weeks he had listened to accounts of the rehearsals, heard discussions about her dresses – more than all, had been saturated in her views of her part. The intensity with which she had expatiated upon subtle points in it recurred to him painfully as he sat in the dress circle and found her to be entirely commonplace. The woman whose dramatic intelligence was so acute in the parlour, displayed not the least touch of inspiration on the stage. She was mediocrity itself. He had a suspicion that Peggy did not think much of her either, although they both applauded loudly.

The journey back was embarrassing to him. They all returned together; and the actress's unconsciousness of having failed to fulfil her conception of the character, her unconsciousness of how piteously far her executive powers fell short of her ideas, made answers to her questions extremely difficult. It was evident, however, that the halting falsehoods which he found himself uttering sounded sincere to her. Again she talked raptly of her reasons for delivering certain lines in a certain way, and the exposition was Admirable – the exposition of an artist; she knew as much about the meaning of the part as the man who had written it. With bewilderment Tatham remembered that the lines when she spoke them had made no impression on him whatever – that the intellect that she had brought to bear upon them would have been suspected by no one – because she couldn't act. It was the truth. She couldn't act. But the fact amazed him.

He would have avoided going in with them when Great Queen Street was reached, but his excuses were overridden. There was a pork pie for supper, large enough for three appetites, and the quantity of beer in the jug showed that his presence at supper had been expected. Well, all the questions had been asked by this time. The party was pleasant enough. The fatigue to which Miss Knight had acknowledged in the tram disappeared at the table; it gave place to high spirits, the hilarity of a woman exhilarated by success. He had never seen her so animated before. The merriment of illusory triumph pealed, and was infectious; by degrees he responded to it, was as talkative as his hostesses. He began to see that Peggy had by now come to feel what she wished to believe; he even ceased to remember that he had been deeply disappointed himself. After all, a first performance was nervous work! It was a scene of light-heartedness, endearments, and self-deception, a scene eminently typical of the world in which it took place.

When Peggy went downstairs to let him out, one o'clock had struck. The staircase and the little shop were quite dark; but for the candle that she carried, he would have been unable to see the way. The responsibility of bolts and chain had been entrusted to her by the householder, and at her bidding he held the candle while she fumbled with them. She appeared to find the task of unfastening the door a complicated one, and for an instant her cheek was so close to his face that all his self-control was necessary. As he strode up the wet street, he kept questioning whether she had given him any credit for the self-control, or thought him merely stupid.

The girl shot the bolts moodily. At least half an hour ago she had decided that he should kiss her when they went downstairs, and the failure of her plan depressed her. Yet she did not think him 'stupid'; she reflected again that he was a 'perfect gentleman'. From his superior point of view, she realised, kissing her would mean a declaration – he couldn't go on coming here and kissing her and never ask her to be engaged to him. Lots of fellows would, of course – all the boys that she knew – just as often as she'd let them, but not Tatham. He wasn't their class. Still, it had been an awful sell! In one way it was a pity a gentleman *was* so particular, for she really was not certain that she wanted to marry him if he did ask her. She wanted him to kiss her, however – she hadn't any doubt about that. Her face was glum when she went back to the room.

'You haven't been very quick about it?' said Naomi Knight, facetiously inquiring.

'Oh, rats!' she snapped.

'Sorry I asked, my pet!'

'I don't know what you mean,' said the girl tartly.

'Nothing to lose your temper about, then, is there?'

'I'm not losing my temper at all. I suppose I can go downstairs to see a pal off without being badgered, can't I? Funny ideas you must have, I'm sure!'

Naomi Knight yawned. 'I think it's time we went to bed. I don't know what's the matter with you all of a sudden.'

'Oh, there's nothing the matter with me,' she exclaimed. 'I'm tired, that's all. I want a cig. Where are they?' She found the remainder of a packet of cheap cigarettes on the mantelpiece, and puffed one violently. 'Oh, Naomi, I am such a fool; I've never been silly about anyone else – I think it's because he's so shy.'

Out of her knowledge, the woman laughed shortly. 'And they fancy we girls are so different from themselves!'

'What's that got to do with it? D'ye think he'll ever say anything?'

'Yes. What are you going to do if he does? You can't marry – I don't suppose he gets thirty bob a week.'

'He's in his uncle's office; surely to goodness he gets more than that? Besides… I don't know. I don't know what I want, that's a fact. I've got the hump.'

'What you want is a jolly long tour; you'd be all right if you didn't see him for a few months.'

'Don't you think I like him?'

'I don't think you're in love with him; you don't care about him really. And if you did, it wouldn't be important at eighteen. Oh, my dear, when one looks back I…What does it amount to afterwards? one can't remember what colour his hair was. Time's rotten. Peg. Time's a beast. There was a fellow – Oh, well!'

'He's writing a play,' said Peggy ruminatively.

'Writing a play? Is he?'

'Of course he hasn't much time, only the evenings. Still authors do make money, don't they?'

'Some of them do. What sort of play is it?'

'A comedy. I – I don't see much in it myself – what he told me. It's about the profession. Who cares about that? The people talk much the same as they do in real life; that's his idea, he wants to be as much like

46

real life as he can. Who cares about real life? And the trouble the plot's giving him! Of course, he must do as he likes, but if I was an author, I'd write costume pieces about bygone times — you don't need to worry about the plot then, any old thing'll do if the people are dressed up quaint and talk old-fashioned. I daresay some costume pieces are all right, but look at most of 'em – my word, the public had got sick of those silly old plots before mother was born! They wouldn't run a night if it wasn't for the clothes and "prithees".'

'I do protest the clothes are monstrous pleasing,' smiled Miss Knight. 'I'd like to read Tatham's piece. Has he shown you any of it? Ask him to lend you the first act if it's finished.'

It was then far from being finished; but when he came again and Peggy said, 'I say, I should like to read your first act when it's done,' the invitation was not one that he was likely to forget.

So, nervously and proudly, a few weeks later he left Act I in her hands for perusal, and spent all the evening picturing her absorbed by it and wondering if he would receive a letter from her by the first post in the morning; and since an account for typewriting was an impossible indulgence before the act received revision, his stack of neat manuscript had been a forbidding object to her when she thanked him.

Naomi Knight found it crumpled behind the sofa cushion next day, where Peggy had forgotten it, after a valiant but vain attempt which petered out at the seventeenth page. She did not own that she had forgotten it; still less would the sentimentality to which she had acknowledged allow her to admit that she had not read it. Her statement that she had 'read it yesterday' and her subsequent pretence of finding the other's opinions of it in agreement with her own was perhaps her earliest affectation.

That her friend happened to be a better critic than an actress was fortunate for Peggy – her Cockney shrewdness took full advantage of the fact. Though she did not deceive the woman for an instant, she deceived the young man continuously. In moments she deceived herself. She was enabled to discuss his work with an assurance that compensated to him for that appalling week during which he had waited, sick with suspense, for a letter that never came. She was at this period a companion to him, and he found nothing remarkable in the circumstances that her objections coincided with Naomi Knight's – it was to be expected that Miss Knight would influence her. Thanks to Miss Knight, she had occasional hints to offer; and again it was by no means astonishing that Miss Knight proved to be of the same mind with regard to them. If the tour of *Mabel, Go and Put On Your Hat* had been extended to the country, Peggy would have been severely embarrassed in her role of dramatic adviser, but it finished at Fulham; and the chief thing that daunted her now was the alarming length of her involuntary vacation. 'Mother's' letter had drawn tears once, when he entered.

"'Tisn't as if she didn't understand!' she quavered. 'She's been out often enough herself; she ought to know it isn't my fault. Great Scott! when I was with Morgan, in panto, she wouldn't have had a cent if it hadn't been for me. I paid all exes right through the season, and took out the muff and chain she'd pawned, too. She's got no right to talk as she does.'

'Oh, well, don't cry,' he said, moved; 'you'll find something soon.'

'I'm not crying. I don't care. She can say what she jolly well likes. Talk about mothers! it's no thanks to her I'm – Oh, well, I know her! she's got out of bed the wrong side, she wrote on one of her days. Next mail I'll get a long letter calling me "Lovey". I'll "lovey" her… She drove father silly! Father was a gentleman. He *was* – father was never in the profession till he married, he only went into it afterwards. He and mother used to run their own companies when I was a kid. I can remember father – he always wore spats. I don't know what's going to become of me! I've had to drop my ads in *The Stage* because I couldn't keep on paying the bob.'

'*I* can find a bob every week,' he said.

'Yes, it'd be *all* right, wouldn't it – you having to give it up yourself and paying for my ads afterwards.'

'Advertising was no use to me anyhow — my name didn't say anything to managers when they saw it.'

'I don't know that it's much use to *me*, if it comes to that. Still, I always do advertise when I've got the money to spare; there's just the chance of your name being seen by someone who's got a vacancy and knows what you can do.'

She consented to write the advertisement presently; and he left it, with a shilling, at *The Stage* office on his way back to the rickety table. The table wobbled under his hand into the small hours now – persistently escaping from the wads of paper that lie placed beneath its legs – and his landlady made an extra charge in the bills for his unconscionable demands upon the gas. Often he took his way to the City sleepily, and it seemed anomalous, now that he grudged each hour there as an encroachment upon precious time, that he was able to fulfil a clerk's duties with a lighter heart. But lighter it was. With the private interest, the new hope to sustain him, he felt more cheerful in the City than he had felt since his initiation. The day might be as gloomy, but the prospect had brightened. There was, in moments, something not unfriendly in the glimpse of the wall and the water-pipe across the red backs of the account books – it was a transparent wall that revealed a future. If the prettiest lines of the dialogue that he had accomplished in the bedroom overnight often intruded next morning when he was perched, casting figures, in the office, their clandestine visit was not without a charm – the office was no sadder for their caress. And his additions weren't much the slower for it.

What Tatham needed pressingly, and had needed pressingly from the moment of his reluctant introduction to hops, was a man's companionship. He was alone. And just as he had exaggerated Peggy in the dreariness of solitude, he exaggerated her now in the eagerness of ambition. Her charm was no longer the mere ray of limelight that she shed – authorship had increased, not diminished, his need of companionship. There were hours – less the hours of difficulty than the effervescent hours of difficulties surmounted – when the society of a man who had the interest to listen and the ability to respond would have been a boon beyond price. A plain young woman, called Naomi Knight, could have supplied all that he in truth sought in Peggy, and have supplied it honestly. But Peggy and she were 'pals' – in their vernacular – so she supplied no more than echoes. And there was another late evening when the dairy and refreshment rooms slumbered when he left.

As it happened, they had not been talking much of his comedy that evening – they had been talking of the letters from Peggy's mother;

for some little time all of them had been written on the lady's 'days' apparently. The girl's eyes were red; she said nothing as she tiptoed down the stairs. In the parlour, only Naomi's presence had prevented a demonstration of his sympathy; in the darkness of the shop he paused, and turned.

'Do buck up, little girl!' he begged, under his breath. 'I hate leaving you like this.'

'I'm all right,' she muttered.

'I wish I could lend you the money, so that you needn't take any from her. You know I haven't got it?'

'What next? Why should you?'

'That isn't it. Do you understand I haven't got it?'

'Of course I understand! Don't look like that; you needn't worry about *me*.'

'I *am* worrying. You don't know how sorry I am for you.'

'Are you?'

Her face was spiritualised in the candlelight, the girlish figure drooped pathetically. He took the candlestick from her hand and put it on the counter, and she didn't ask him 'why.'

'Peggy!' he exclaimed – and she was sobbing on his shoulder.

'Don't, kiddy! I love you.'

She sobbed more unrestrainedly. He stroked her hair, and kissed her on the cheek, stammering empty phrases of encouragement. Empty as they were, they calmed her – she was smiling when she raised her head. 'I love you,' he said again, thinking it true, and kissed her on the lips.

After the silence, 'I don't care *now!*' she said. She was radiant, though her lashes glistened. She stood at arm's length from him, regarding him triumphantly.

'Will you wait till we can marry?'

Quick nods gave answer.

'Even if it's a long time? It will be a long time, Peggy.'

'I expect it will.'

'You see, I'm not alone, I've got to help my mother; my salary doesn't do much for me.'

'Lot o' mothers, aren't there?' she pouted playfully. 'There's the comedy!'

'Oh yes, if I get the comedy taken, if it's a success, we shall be as right as rain!.. You'll give up the stage then, won't you? I don't want you to go on acting when we're married.'

'"When we are mar-ried,"' she hummed from *The Belle of New York*. 'Oh, I'll give it up, never fear!

When we are mar-ried,
What will you do?
I'll be so tender and faithful to you –

'Are those the right words? They sound good enough, don't they?'

'They sound lovely,' he cried. But there was something lacking in his tone.

'Sh! don't talk so loud, we shall wake Mrs Tucker; she sleeps down-stairs.' She laughed softly. 'Things do change, don't they – who'd have thought five minutes ago? Naomi won't know me when I go back!'

'What'll she say? Will she –'

'What?'

'Say you're foolish?'

'She knows that already.'

'What – about me? Why, does she guess, then?'

'What do *you* think? Naomi thought you liked me the first time you came. Did you?'

'Of course I did,' he said, though he couldn't remember very clearly. He was conscious of feeling less emotion than he would have expected, conscious of being more self-possessed. He kissed her again, to stimu-late his ardour. 'Well, is she against it?'

'Why should she be?'

'Only the waiting.'

'Oh, well, I'm not in a hurry! Leastwise –'

He winced, and despised himself for wincing while her arms were round his neck. 'You *should* be in a hurry,' he said, humorously indignant.

'Well, I won't put it off when you're ready. How's that?'

'That's better. And you won't get tired of being engaged to me, either? It'll be the longest "engagement" you've ever had!'

'I say, I can write and tell mother I've found one at last! Now ask me if mother's going to be against it. It'd make a lot of difference if she was. But won't it suit her all right to get somebody to take me off her hands! Best bit of luck that's come mother's way for a long time.'

He said meditatively, 'I don't think I shall like your mother.'

'I'll bet you do! – if you don't see too much of her. She's much more popular in a company than I am – till the tour's about half over. Then she generally has rows. I never knew mother to say "no" to a subscription – she's awfully good-natured to strangers… What about yours? She won't be keen on it, will she?'

'I don't know why she should mind; we aren't together as it is. It won't make any difference to what I do for her… I suppose I ought to say "good night"?'

'I suppose so,' she assented grudgingly, 'or we shall have Naomi coming down to see what we're up to. Hullo! the candle's going out; it'll be blind man's holiday.'

'Can you manage the door?…. I'll come up with you and get another light. Yes, I'll go up again, too – then we can tell her together. I think I'd like to do that.'

'Would you? What for?'

'I think I'd better do that,' he said.

The wick of the candle stump had dropped; the china glowed redly for a moment, and then faded out of view. She put her hand on his, cautioning him to 'mind the step', enjoining him 'not to make a noise'. Naomi was standing by the parlour mantelpiece, taking down her hair, and jerked round as she saw his reflection in the glass.

'You needn't mind *him*,' cried Peggy hilariously, 'we're engaged!'

VII

He presented her with a ring a few days later – a pitiful ring that he never noticed on her finger without humiliation – and his watch had departed from him again, this time with the chain attached. His cousin Harold was recently engaged, and once when Tatham went to No. 12 he saw the fiancée and the diamond she was wearing, and pitied Peggy quite superfluously. To her own eyes his trumpery gift looked intrinsically important.

He had not been to No. 12 often since he was a clerk in the office – the inquiry, 'Shall we see you on Sunday?' was made at long, and longer intervals – and he did not deem it essential to announce his love affair to his relatives. By this time he had begun to question whether he inspired quite so warm a sense of satisfaction in his uncle as he had imagined at the start, and discretion hinted that he was not likely to increase approval by talking of matrimony. He did not mention the subject, either, when he wrote to Sweetbay.

His labour on the comedy he had kept secret from the first. The Spauldings, he conjectured, would disapprove of it, now that he belonged to hops, and his mother would ask in every letter – long before the rough draft was finished – 'what day his piece was to be produced'. The delays and rejections that he foresaw would be bitter enough in any case – there was no necessity to make them bitterer. To the domestic circle of the amateur a rejected manuscript proclaims him inept and vain. The amateur's family is unaware that in the literature of the world there is no masterpiece which would not have been rejected in one quarter or another if judged solely on its merits.

Yes, he meant to spare himself that. Only in Great Queen Street they heard his alternate hopes and discouragements while the manuscript grew bulkier, and by no means always were his moods confided there. Far more frequently were Peggy's affairs the topic. Within a fortnight of the engagement her outlook brightened.

'You've been lucky to me,' she exclaimed one day; 'I've had an offer!'

She had obtained a part in a company that was to give its opening performance in the Midlands, and proceed distressfully northward.

'You call that "luck"?' he complained, when she had rattled details.

'Oh, well, we shall be at Croydon for the last week; you'll be able to see me there!' Her glance was very tender, but her gaiety jarred him a little. He had to remind himself that one must expect an actress to be happy at separation in such circumstances.

'When is it you go to Croydon?'

'I don't know exactly,' she said; 'I haven't got all the dates. I know we do go there for the last week, because I asked which was our nearest point to London. It's supposed to be a three months' tour – that means, it'll be about eleven weeks before I see you. Rotten, isn't it?'

'It isn't very jolly. If I weren't so hard up I could go down to you for weekends.'

'Wouldn't that be all right! Well, you'll have to come round and talk to Naomi instead. I say! don't you go making up to Naomi while I'm away or there'll be trouble. My word!'

'Don't talk like that!'

'Oh, well, perhaps she is a bit too old for you! – I wouldn't trust you if she was my age, take it from *me*. If you were here too much while I was gone it'd be all up with you, young man – I'd ask Mrs Tucker how long you'd stayed and give you jip.' She leant towards him, laughing, coquettish, amused by her own spring of humour.

He went with her and Naomi to St Pancras on a Sunday morning to say *au revoir* at the latest moment possible, and he found it strange to watch actors and actresses again straggling up a station platform, and to loiter by the window of a compartment labelled 'Reserved: *No Child to Call Her 'Mother'* Co.' He was very sorry that she was going; he was conscious that he would miss her acutely; already London presented in his thoughts some of the vast forlornness that had intimidated him before his meeting with her in Long Acre; but, though he didn't recognise the fact, and would have been ashamed to perceive it, the prevailing melancholy of his mood was not a lover's. She was bound for the life that he had left! As he stood there, waiting for the train to start, sentiment had reached the journey's end. Situations sordid in actuality were beautified, not by remembrance merely, by temperament itself. Emotional to realise how far she and her companions were about to travel from him – in less than two hours they would have reached another world!

'I'll send you a postcard tomorrow, old boy,' she exclaimed, bending forward, but not lowering her voice. Outside, he smiled and nodded. From what incalculable remoteness would the postcard come!

Naomi had more to say to her than he while they waited. There was a moment in which he realised wistfully that he would never desire to confide to her what the scene had made him feel, a revealing moment in which he longed for somebody who would have understood. He was, however, leagues from realising that not one person in a multitude would have understood, or beheld more than a posse of ill-mannered persons departing for a tawdry sphere.

'Take your seats there, please!'

Girls thrust their heads through the windows of the labelled compartments, with final injunctions. She called to Naomi, 'Don't forget to send on my blouse – and mind, I shan't pay her for washing it, because of the things she's lost!' She blew a kiss to him. 'So long!' On the platform, hands were waved. One enthusiast flourished a dirty handkerchief. No man but Tatham took off his hat.

'Eleven weeks'll soon go by,' said Naomi for comfort, as they turned.

'Oh yes,' he concurred feebly.

'It'd have been nice if she could have got something to do in town. But that's so difficult.'

'Of course. Yes, I shall miss her. So will you, I suppose? I know, she'll always be going away – I shall have to get used to it.'

They walked out of the station, along the Sunday morning dullness of the streets. She was removing, for financial reasons, to other lodgings Mrs Tucker having objected to 'cut up her let'.

'It'd have done you good to have someone to talk to while she was gone,' she said; 'but I can't ask you to come round, because I shall only have one room.'

'I know,' he answered. 'I'm sorry.' Peggy had told him that, affecting humorously to be much relieved. 'Yes, I shall be pretty lonely without you both; it'll be as bad as ever, and worse.'

It was as bad as ever as soon as they had separated. Doughty Street looked desolate. He spent the afternoon re-reading his manuscript – he had no heart to continue writing it – and wondered again if it was destined to open a career to him, and how long he must expect to wait for the verdict from the Pall Mall Theatre, where he meant to send it first.

The manuscript was now the only company that he had on any evening. There was no one for him to rush to, exultant, on the great night when the play was finished at last and he believed that never, were he to write for years, could he do better work than this that lay accomplished on the table. That other people might do so he admitted, but not he – it was the best of which he would ever be capable! His gaze dwelt approvingly on the last words that he had traced. Not so long ago he had foreseen his last words scribbled at white heat on the final page; they had been inserted with meticulous deliberation on page 3 – an insignificant amendment to which he had devoted an hour's consideration. No, there was no one for him to tell; but the attic penned him, and, going out for a brisk turn round Mecklenburgh Square, he tramped excitedly to Hampstead Heath.

One benefit had accrued to him from Peggy's absence – he had been enabled to store shillings in sufficient numbers to face the outlay for type-writing that was necessary; all the morning his manuscript lay concealed in the City, and he sped with it to a typist in the luncheon hour. The sensation of the 'double life' was overwhelming.

And when he had nerved himself to sully the imposing neatness of that typescript by copperplate corrections, when it had been wrapped in a new sheet of brown paper, and directed painstakingly and he handed it across a post office counter, there was a little thrill in the reflection that the girl who registered it must reverently guess he was a dramatist.

'What time will it be delivered?' he asked her.

'Oh, some time this afternoon,' said the girl shortly.

She pitched his comedy into a basket.

BOOK II

I

Thanks to the ease with which human nature can avert its eyes from the uncomplimentary, Time is referred to exclusively as the 'healer'. That it is the cynic that mocks love, friendship, ideals, and various virtues, believed to be lifelong while they absorb us, we prefer to ignore. Time – no larger a slice of it than three years – had taught Christopher Tatham to remember his first comedy, when he remembered it at all, with amused contempt. The emotions that it had brought were dead. He marvelled that once he had been so absurd as to fancy the work was good. In fine, though he was still a clerk, aspiring vainly to prove himself a playwright, Christopher Tatham had learnt a good deal of his craft. But the emotions that he scorned had been Youth – and Time, the double-faced, had taken while it gave.

Marriage, often discussed, was still a distant prospect. His income remained ridiculously inadequate to support a mother and a wife as well. This, despite a recent increase in his salary. Once the girl had proposed that she should 'keep on acting' after they married, but, even so, she would depend on his support during more than half the year, for her own salaries were, not merely few, but pitifully small. Once, too, oppressed by the gloom of the outlook, he had offered to release her from her promise; her blithe refusal of his proffered sacrifice had, in truth, rejoiced him less than he wished to think.

Of the attitude of Mrs Harper, now that he had at last met her, Tatham was far from complaining. Her professional sojourn in Australia had been prolonged so much beyond the period foreseen that she had returned to London, cheerful with brief prosperity, only a few months since. Facing a presentation that he would gladly have avoided, he had met, to his relief, a stout, merry little woman, whose informal welcome had banished his restraint almost at once. Cordial to him on his first visit, she now appeared to entertain for him feelings that approached affection; and never had he witnessed in her manner towards her daughter anything to explain the girl's earlier comments upon her. On the contrary, he had occasionally been jarred in noting a lack of suavity in Peggy's tone towards her mother.

'Oh, because mother's taken to you, you think she's an angel,' said the girl a shade sullenly, when he dropped a hint to her on the subject. 'She's a good deal better since she's been back, but she's no treat to live with, all the same, I give you my word!'

The three years had made little change in Peggy Harper. She had still the same girlish, rather vacuous expression, the same lithe slip of a figure. Professionally she asserted that she was eighteen, and so young did she look, and so constantly was the assertion repeated, that Tatham often noted with amusement that she and her mother had come near to believing it. When he was lamenting his position to Mrs Harper one afternoon – he had found her alone – 'Why, Peggy's only a child,' she laughed. 'Bless the boy, you needn't worry about the "waiting" yet; if you don't get married for five years to come, there'll be plenty of time left for your matrimonial squabbles. What is it you're frightened of – somebody else running off with her?'

'I'm not frightened; I'm depressed,' he said.

'Care killed a cat.

Laugh, and the world laughs with you;
Weep, and you weep alone!'

She quoted with over-emphasis, but feeling, and paused questioningly, as if for an audience to applaud her. 'You aren't the first author that's had the hump. They've all had to go through the same thing – the best of them. And, take it from me, it was never so easy for a young writer to get a chance on the stage as it is today.'

'Easy?' His mind's eye saw forlornly into a corner drawer, where tattered comedies lay. He looked round the long circle that each of them had travelled, growing gradually shabbier, till it had been buried in the corner drawer at last. 'It was never so expensive as it is today; I wish the typewriter hadn't been invented!'

She nodded. 'I've seen a bit. Lord! twenty-five, thirty years ago, when they used to say there was a "dramatic ring", you could count the dramatists on one hand. Nobody else had a look in. They didn't give a new man a chance in those days, not once in a blue moon. Now, why, they produce go-as-you-please plays by amateurs all over the shop! You don't have to know anything like as much about your business, to get a piece produced now, as you had to know when I was a girl. I can tell you that, young man!' She was suddenly self-important; the sharpness of vexation in her voice made him wonder what he had said to annoy her. 'Don't you run away with the idea that, because Betsy Harper isn't a star, she's never known anything better than the kind of crowds you see her play in now! Well, you *haven't* seen me play yet, but you shall, some time, if you're good. I want you to see me in a good part, the first time you do come – a Mrs John Wood part, that's my line. My God! if somebody'd write me a part like Lady Twombley in *The Cabinet Minister* I'd make things hum! No, don't you run away with that idea, Master Tatham. There was a time,

> *There was a time when all I touched turned gold,*
> *When friends flocked merrily to taste my bounty!*

You don't know who wrote that? Clement Scott. Let me see. It was when he was editing *The Theatre*. *That* wasn't yesterday. You were in your cradle.

> *I never turned a dog into the cold,*
> *Nor let the poor go starving to the County.*

Yes, there was a time when I knew people who've gone to the top since then. *I've* heard 'em talk! Millington used to come in to supper with us, long before his burlesques were the rage – when he was selling pen'orths of pins over his father's counter in Camden Town. *He* had something to say, too. Worse than you, he was. I remember his first pantomime, one Christmas Eve, in Birmingham – awful mess he made of it! He came to dinner with us the next day and opened the window and wanted to throw himself out. We had to hang on to him for a quarter of an hour, with the snow blowing in on the goose. I know' – she beamed at him, with a world of meaning – 'authors can't help it; you're a rotten lot, every one of you – all hump before you get on, and all swelled head afterwards. When you've had a West End run, *you'll* swank over better men than yourself. Yes, you, my modest violet!'

'Don't you believe it. If I ever do get a West End run, I shall remember what I've been through.'

'Oh, you'll remember right enough. Trust you! They all remember, that's what makes them so damned offensive – they want to get a bit of their own back. Authors? If I didn't like you such a lot, I'd never be fool enough to let Peggy marry an author, I'd rather see her marry an actor – and that's saying something. Oh, I met somebody who knows you this week – Galbraith.'

'Galbraith!' he exclaimed. 'Do you know him? How is he?'

'Do I know him?' echoed Betsy Harper.

'These kids asking me if I know Galbraith! I knew him before London knew him. I knew Galbraith when his part was "The carriage waits, my lord." If you come in and have a bit of steak with us on Sunday evening you'll see him.'

It was in North Crescent, Bloomsbury, where the Harpers were lodging, that his Sunday evenings were generally spent now; and there on the Sunday following he met the actor to whom he had once confided his fear of being compelled to leave 'the profession'. Galbraith's sparse hair was whiter, his shoulders drooped a little more, but it seemed to Tatham that the refined, clean-shaven face had altered not at all. Very few persons, ignorant of the man's vice, would have suspected it by his appearance, which, thanks to the long intervals of rigid abstinence, remained a gentleman's.

'So you hadn't forgotten me, Galbraith. It's a long time ago!'

'I didn't know you'd ever been in a crowd with Galbraith,' chirruped Peggy. 'You never told me. When was it?'

'In the brave days when we were twenty-one,' said Galbraith, 'eh? Of course, we were the bright particular stars, Tatham and I! Do you remember that beautiful, soul-stirring bit of bombast, Tatham, that always brought a round when I took a step back and looked at the gallery?'

'I daresay I remember it better than you do by now,' laughed Tatham.

'I shouldn't wonder – I've spouted such a lot of stuff just as rotten since. Betsy, when you played "Nan" and I was "Young Mr Simpson", and thought you a great actress – the illusions of youth –'

'Hit him for me, somebody!' said Mrs Harper.

'Why did you, with the giddy impulse of a kindly heart, encourage me to persevere on a path that has led me to the slough of second-class shows in third-class towns? Now, you've done better by this fellow, you've taken him off it!'

'Me?' she cried.

'Oh, that wasn't mother!'

'Oh, that wasn't "mother"? I thought it sounded practical for Betsy!'

'That was the mother of invention – I got off it while Mrs Harper was shining in Australia.'

'I did shine, too, don't make any mistake about that! I wish I'd stopped there – I don't see much chance over here. Know anybody who wants me, Galbraith?'

Galbraith smiled pensively. '*He'll* be writing parts for us all by-and-by! Don't forget me, your old pal, Tatham. Give me a nice comfortable part with nothing to do in the last act, so that I can get home to bed early. I'm not greedy any more, I don't want to be in the picture at the end; a part that's the centre of attraction for three acts, and carries a big salary, will be good enough for me today.'

'Who told you he was writing? Mother, of course. She would!' said the girl tartly.

'And why shouldn't I? Is it a State secret?'

'"Mother, of course"! Why not? Is there any particular reason why he shouldn't be told?'

'Talking about things before there's anything to say! That's just mother. If you hear of an off-chance of a part, it's "Peggy's going out to play it!" I don't believe in counting your chickens before they're hatched, nor does Chris; it's unlucky.'

'Oh, telling Galbraith isn't counting chickens,' he interposed hurriedly; 'he understands. I'm one of the Great Unacted, Galbraith, that's all. Do you ever come across anybody I know, any of the people who were with us? I never see any of them advertise. By the way, what's Miss Knight doing now, Peggy?'

'Naomi? She was going out with some show or other, the last time she was here. I suppose she's on tour. I hope so; things have been awful with her.'

'She's got no talent,' observed Mrs Harper; 'she can't act for nuts, that young woman. I don't know how she expects to do any good.'

Tatham remembered Naomi Knight making a similar comment upon others.

'I don't know how anybody expects to do any good, if it comes to that. I'd rather be anywhere than on the stage, myself,' returned her daughter; and the servant, who had come in with the steak, showed no surprise. They were in 'professional apartments', and she had overheard the sentiments of more than one actress in her time.

'Help yourself to beer, Galbraith.'

'No beer for me today,' said Galbraith casually, 'I'll have water – I've had a touch of liver.'

'Oh, go on, a glass of beer won't hurt you!' exclaimed the hostess.

'What do you press him for, mother, when he says it isn't good for him?' remonstrated the girl sharply – much too sharply for her to sound ignorant of the truth. 'Will you have some soda, Galbraith? Chris, you might bring that syphon over.'

It was acutely painful to Tatham to know the man fearful even to taste ale lest it should inflame his tendency to excess; but Galbraith, who was once more strictly virtuous, owing to a recent disaster, seemed to sup cheerfully enough. It was not till he and Tatham were alone – they left North Crescent together – that a sigh escaped him.

'Very tactless of Betsy at supper, Tatham,' he said, 'what?'

'You mean –'

'Persuading me to take beer. It's awkward enough to have to refuse; and then when they argue with you besides! If kind friends'd only take "no" for an answer, when I'm behaving myself, I shouldn't lose so many shops. It's a funny thing, though, you know, if I had taken a glass or two this evening, it wouldn't have led to any ill results. It's only when I'm in an engagement that I can't stop. I can take a drink as rationally as anybody else when I haven't got to be at the theatre at night; I know when I've had enough then just as well as you do. But – it's a most mysterious thing – the moment a salary depends on my keeping sober, a single drop is absolutely fatal to me; it's like the taste of blood to a tiger. Very curious, Tatham, very remarkable that a man should be without self-control only at the times when he has the strongest reasons for controlling himself? When I was at the Diadem, when I was getting good terms, I once paid a specialist two guineas just to put that point to him. He said it was 'very extraordinary'. Of course, I knew that myself. I can't make it out. Because it isn't as if I were a wastrel and didn't care whether I was sacked or not – it goes to my heart to think of the chances I've thrown away. Nobody despises me when I lose a shop so much as I despise myself. I'm so disgusted with my weakness that I can't look at myself when I'm shaving – and yet there it is! Still, Betsy shouldn't persuade me; it'd do her no harm to take to barley-water.'

'What?' said Tatham, staring round at him.

'Didn't you know? Oh yes, Betsy's slightly inclined that way – or she used to be; I don't know how it is with her today.'

Tatham kept pace with him sickly. This, then, was what the girl had meant by saying that she had much to put up with. An immense pity for Peggy engulfed him. a pity for Mrs Harper. Questions, misgivings eddied in his mind during the five seconds before Galbraith spoke again.

'I don't mean that she's like *me*,' added the actor in a tone profoundly contemptuous of himself; 'nothing to – Well, you're engaged to the girl! That's all right. Betsy isn't a "bad case". I wouldn't have mentioned it if I'd guessed you didn't know. I'm sorry I let it slip.'

'You needn't be. Poor little Peggy! She must have a rough time. I wish I could take her out of it. I'm so frightfully hard up.'

'In the City,' said Galbraith, 'aren't you?'

'In the City? In a clerkship! I haven't got a thing to look forward to if I don't strike oil writing. I shall soon have been at it for four years! I suppose "four years" doesn't sound long to the man who listens, but it sounds a long time to the man who works – and hasn't got anything to show for it, except plays that no one'd have.'

'Tolmore was writing for the best part of twenty before he did any good. I used to go in and smoke a pipe with him when they lived in Featherstone Buildings. Jolly good chap he was then. They've got a flat in Pont Street now, and he looks the other way when he sees me in the Strand. I suppose you haven't got a drama up your sleeve, have you?'

'Why? Do you know anybody who'd take one from me?' His voice was fervid. 'I could write one! I've only done comedies, hut I'd write a drama, if there were half a chance.'

'Well, people'll take my recommendations much sooner than they'll take *me*, you know. I might get Logan Ross to read it; I know he wants another drama to tour with. Of course,' he laughed, 'you know what it'd have to be?'

'The kind of thing I used to play in, I suppose?'

'I expect he'd want something more sensational than that – they're Olivers for sensation now. In the country you can't give them too much of it. You might make some money – if he'd pay royalties – but there'd be no kudos – except among the Logan Rosses; I suppose *they'd* think it clever if it drew the public.'

'I've *got* to make some money,' said Tatham doggedly. 'I'll take any job that anybody'll give me. That's the right point of view, isn't it? I wouldn't sit down to write muck deliberately if I had any choice, but if I don't write, I don't do anything at all – the City's a cul-de-sac. I can stick as I am for years to come, I'm tired of it, I'm ashamed of it… Is it any use my dropping a line to him?'

'I'd better look him up,' said Galbraith; 'he wouldn't answer a letter. I'll have a chat with the gentleman. Then, if he's on, you can go and see him yourself. You'll have to go with an idea, you know – it's no use your talking about a play if you've nothing to propose— and I shouldn't tell him you write comedies; don't mention the West End – that'd be nearly as fatal as if you had had a success there. Tell him you've an "inspiration for a money-maker" – that'll be expressive to Ross — and then gas about your biggest thrill. I don't know what there is left to think of, myself, but if you can strike something that hasn't been done yet, you'll hold his attention. Of course, there's the risk of his sneaking your idea and passing it on to an author he knows, but he's pretty decent for a mummer.'

His voice was suddenly plaintive. 'Between ourselves, Tatham! I shouldn't have said that; I think it's caddish to foul one's own nest… Where are you staying?'

They stopped under a lamppost while the young man pencilled his address on a scrap of paper – he had recently removed to Berners Street;

and before they separated, Galbraith undertook to attend to the matter on the morrow. As Tatham continued his way, however, his thoughts dwelt less on the dramatic prospect than on the domestic revelation. He had not been engaged for three years without realising that he wasn't in love with Peggy; but he had been conscious that he had a duty to her. Heavily it seemed to him that his duty had never been so strong as now. He was pledged to marry her one day; he meant to marry her one day. The sooner the day came, then, the better – for her, at any rate!... A rough-and-tumble drama? It would be a far stride from the delicate comedies in the drawer, comedies which, Mrs Harper always told him, had the defect of being insufficiently theatrical. Still, Hobson's choice – assuming he were fortunate enough to gain the chance at all! And mightn't it be possible to introduce some human nature even into a rough-and-tumble drama?

II

The promise that Galbraith had made was the kind of promise that many more reputable persons in his profession, and out of it, would promptly have forgotten; Galbraith, who had broken vows innumerable towards himself, kept his word. A few days later, Tatham was de- lighted to receive a note advising him to call on Mr Ross the following evening, and he had in the interval evolved an idea which, if devoid of startling novelty, was unhackneyed enough to justify the visit. His hope of palli- ating a crude subject by the treatment that he gave to it, he decided to suppress in the interview.

Mr Logan Ross's house – he referred to it as his 'residence' – was situated in Loughborough Road, and was furnished with no little comfort. He was an indifferent actor, even judged by the standard of a bad school, but as a manager he had been blessed with an instinct for providing what his public wanted. Thanks to that inestimable gift, he had made money. Of such plays as he occasionally witnessed in the fashionable theatres of London he understood no more than he under- stood of literature or the contents of the National Gallery; but, now that instinct had been supplemented by experience, he understood, as accurately as any one man can ever do, at what point in his own dramatic fare an audience of the lower middle class would shuffle their feet and want a crime to happen – at what point their appetites would turn from crime to sentiment; he understood how often, in the menu of love and murder, the savoury desired by every palate would be for the low comedian to sit down on an egg.

To such a manager, the author of comedies that were too untheatrical for their cleverness to make speedy converts had arrived to propose a melodrama!

And the proposal found favour. It was, on the face of it, a thing almost as strange as any that had happened in Mr Logan Ross's most popular productions. The applicant had been appraised in five minutes, and found wanting; the expert had cast his large body into an armchair and stretched his legs on his hearth with an unconcealed yawn. Melodrama was a science, and he was listening to an amateur! The story had opened well enough in some respects, but it was off the beaten track, and the beaten track was where the money lay – he didn't contemplate prospecting. And then there had come one nervous swerve of originality, which the applicant himself esteemed less highly than much that had preceded it, and the eye of experience saw suddenly the glitter of gold. This young man couldn't do justice to his notion; but he, Ross, could do justice to it – *he* could cut and paste and pull the situations closer together; *he* could knock out all the reasons why people did things and make them go and do 'em quick! A novice with fresh ideas might be worth cultivating, after all.

He maintained a discouraging silence when the author finished speaking… 'Humph!' he grunted at last.

'You don't care for it?' said Tatham, trying to sound indifferent.

'I don't say there isn't anything in it,' admitted Ross, in the tone of a man seeking to be generous, and paused again.

Tatham's idea of the value of what he had to sell was falling fast. 'Of course, I've told it badly,' he murmured.

'I don't say there isn't anything in it,' repeated Ross; 'some of it's all right, but – I don't know – I don't know – Galbraith's a dear old pal of mine, nobody's enemy but his own – but I'll be perfectly plain with you, my dear chap. I can't talk about a play that isn't written. I can't say anything tonight. Galbraith ought to know that. If you had put four acts in front of me I could give you an answer; I could say, "It's no use to me" or "It's a go". You know what a production by me means – people are going to tumble over one another to see it. The respect's not all on one side – *I've* got to be very careful what I give 'em… Look here, bring me your play complete, and if I like it, I do it!'

'What terms would you pay for it?'

'My dear boy,' said Ross engagingly, 'I'll be as open as the day with you. If I like it, we shan't quarrel about terms; if I'm not keen on it, I wouldn't have it as a gift. I can't say more than that. I can't settle terms till I've seen the thing. I suppose you could knock it off in a couple of months, eh?'

'What?'

'I don't know when it would be of any use to *me* if you didn't – I'll want to start rehearsing in a couple of months… Well, say three, at the outside.'

There were cigarettes and whisky and soda before he left. He left exhilarated, persuaded that, after all, three months was a long time – Ross, who hadn't to create the manuscript, had cheerfully insisted that it was a long time – and it did not shrink affrightingly until some hours later. When it had begun to shrink, he was surprised to discover how remote the conclusion of the next three months appeared to everyone who hadn't the work to do. Galbraith assured him that he could 'do it on his head by then', and Peggy echoed, 'three months!' as if it were an effort to project the imagination to a date so distant.

'I say,' she exclaimed happily on another occasion, 'you'll be able to get me a shop! If Ross takes the piece, mind you tell him he's to give me an engagement in it.'

'Yes, write a good part for Peggy,' chuckled her mother. 'And don't forget Ma! What's the use of having an author in the family if he doesn't pull wires for us. What *I* want is a part like "Lady Twombley" so now you know; *I'll* make your piece a success for you!' Then, as she saw his embarrassment, 'I'm only joking,' she laughed. 'Think you're talking to an amateur? Don't I know you can't shape your play to suit everybody?'

'I daresay I could manage something for Peggy,' he said, ruminating. 'I'd like to do it for *you*, if I could… I'd like to do something for Galbraith.'

'Don't you make a fool of yourself!' she cried. 'Well, Ross wouldn't have him, if you tried it on, but don't you go asking for trouble. We all know what Galbraith's little weakness is. You'd look lively if he turned up helpless on your first night. No sentiment in business, my son – take it from one who knows. Now give Peggy a kiss and go home to your scribbling. If you're stuck on Sunday, you can come round and have supper with us; and if you're busy, we shan't expect you.'

She would not, as his mother-in-law, win approbation at No. 12 – assuming that his uncle and aunt ever invited her there – he knew it with a qualm, just as he knew what they would think of Peggy if they ever saw her; but, whatever her faults might be, he found her very human. And when he did run round to North Crescent for half an hour now, it was Betsy Harper, not her girl, who showed the livelier interest in hearing what his progress had been. It was she, not the girl, who had sometimes a useful word to say. It occurred to him distressfully more than once that it was she, too, who understood better what it meant to him to leave for the office every morning under a weight that threatened to crush him – not as a clerk, whose undistinguished duties had become more or less mechanical, but as an author whose desperate strokes were stemming the rush of time. And this vulgar and intemperate little woman did understand it better than her daughter, was indeed vividly sympathetic in a situation where many far superior persons would have seen nothing but a very ordinary young man engaged in the prosaic task of trying to make a living. As a woman she did not complain of his being natural – she complained of it only as a reader.

It was unfortunate that impulse took him to the house on a certain afternoon. Her greeting was less cordial on that day.

'Hullo! Peggy's out,' she said.

'Is she? What a nuisance!' But if he was sorry to miss her, his regret was not so acute that it damped his anticipation of a pleasant half-hour. 'What time will she be back?'

'Now you're asking!' said Mrs Harper with umbrage. 'When it suits her ladyship, I suppose. It's not for me to be told what time she'll be back. There are daughters and daughters! Do you know that, Mr Tatham, Esquire?'

'Well, I suppose there are,' he murmured uncomfortably. 'Peggy's a very nice one, though. You think so too.'

She regarded him for a moment in surly silence: 'I think so too? That's a funny thing to say. How do you know what I think? Eh?'

'Well, I hope you think so, Mrs Harper. May I put it like that?' He had taken a seat opposite her, and he got up, paling. Her condition was evident; he was consumed by a desire to escape without seeming to her abrupt. 'I can't stop – I only ran in for a moment to see how you were both getting on.'

She took no notice of this; she repeated with rising cantankerousness, 'How do you know what I think? I suppose, because you're an author, you fancy you know all about everything, don't you? An author?' Her laugh was derisive. 'A fine author *you* are!'

'Very eminent, I know! We needn't argue that point.'

'Argue?' Again her slow stare was resentful. '*I* don't argue with *you*. A woman like me argue with you? That's a very impertinent remark!

I don't *argue* with you; I don't pay you such a compliment. I tell you what I've got to say, I don't argue with you. Who are *you*? I take no insults from anybody.'

'Insult?' he stammered. 'Mrs Harper… Well, we'll talk about it another time.'

'Oh, dear me! "We'll talk about it another time" – spoken with dignity – the actor crosses the stage! Perhaps there won't be any "other time", my lord duke; that's for *me* to say. These are my rooms, I think? I pay for these rooms, don't I? – and just who I choose comes to them, and nobody else. D'ye see?' The quiet insolence of her tone shrilled to passion. She was all at once a prey to violent, unreasoning rage. 'You come here at my good pleasure. If you don't behave yourself, you don't set foot in the place again! D'ye hear that? I won't have you here; I won't let Peggy marry you. Who are you – you and your plays? Do you think she's going to spend her life waiting for you? A girl like her could do better for herself tomorrow than marry a chap like *you*!'

'That's so. If Peggy feels the same way about it, she's quite free.'

'Oh, is she?' She paused; her views veered; there was infinite meaning in her alcoholic bitterness. 'I *dare* say. Well, take care you don't get a breach of promise case, Mr. High-and-Mighty, that's all! You can't play fast and loose with a girl of mine, don't you believe it. Not much you can't! A good girl she is, a long sight too good for *you*! If she'd taken my advice, she'd have sent you to the right-abouts long ago.' She screamed, she was hideous; her invective pursued him to the staircase.

It was unfortunate because neither of them ever contrived to banish the restraint that the occurrence caused. They tried to talk as if the scene were forgotten when, at Peggy's solicitation, he went to the house again; but on the man's side there was misgiving, and on the woman's there was shame, and the familiar tone of confidence was never successfully re-established. 'I can only ask you to think that mother wasn't well,' the girl had pleaded. And he had kissed her very tenderly, moved by the undesigned pathos of the words – conscience-stricken, too, in realising all that had underlain his retort that she was free if she wished their engagement at an end.

It was at this stage that the ordinary young man ceased to make illusions for himself. He no longer strove to stifle repentance with the assertion that 'though he wasn't in love, he was very fond of her.' He knew that the tenderness of his kiss had been the tenderness of pity; he saw clearly that he had blundered the night that he kissed her first. But he was honourable, or weak enough – the epithet varies with the point of view – to believe that he would be a cad to own it to her. She had waited for him so long; she had waited because he had asked her to wait! The knowledge burdened him. That he had been very young when he asked her, that, in looking back, he seemed to have been amazingly young and mindless, even for his age, could not liberate him, he felt. Ethically, perhaps, he would be doing her a greater wrong to marry her than to confess the truth; but conventionally, the worse offence would be to tell her so late that he didn't care for her. And she would think he was throwing her over because her mother drank. Horrible to make a girl feel that! Horrible also to realise that, after marriage, he must often expect to find the mother quarrelsome in her cups!

III

When the drama for Mr Logan Ross was delivered – it had been accomplished within three atrocious months – Mr Logan Ross's pressing need of it had evidently subsided. Some weeks passed before he had leisure to read it. Communicating curtly with the author at last, he offered to buy the work outright for ten pounds. And after an interval of blind fury, the author with equal curtness accepted the offer.

'At any rate,' Galbraith had said, 'you get your foot in – it's a production. However rotten the price was, I shouldn't try to stand out for terms with a first play.' And Mrs Harper had remembered someone, subsequently celebrated, who sold his first comedy for a pound per act.

Yes, in view of all the circumstances, it was probably as much as he would be able to command in any quarter, so the offer was accepted. And his chief desire now was to receive the cheque and never to be reminded of his melodrama again.

The hopes that he had built on it were dust; he told himself that he didn't care a curse for the thing any more. He had cared in writing it, had in hours found it absorbing, even while he called himself a fool for the pains he was taking to embroider shoddy; his efforts to redeem the plot by characterisation had been too strenuous for him to be able to regard the manuscript simply as a potboiler. But deliberately he had chosen a plot opposed to his tastes and written to make money. And he was offered ten pounds! He soliloquised about Logan Ross, impugning his integrity; he said, with perfect justice, that a piece must be worth more than ten pounds to be worth anything at all. He told the walls of the bedroom in Berners Street that the manager whom *The Wigan Examiner* described as 'a powerful and romantic actor' was a strongly qualified thief. With that lack of business intelligence which Mr Spaulding deplored in him, he failed to differentiate between clumsy or penal dishonesty and dishonesty on safe or commercial lines. He was happy to reflect that Mr Logan Ross would have the impudence to seek no interview, after their exchange of epistolary brevities.

Mr Ross, in the least embarrassed manner imaginable, wrote asking him to call 'with regard to a few slight changes in the script'.

And as the cheque wasn't enclosed in the letter he swallowed his indignation and went.

So frank and free was the manager's greeting that he seemed leagues from suspecting indignation. Indeed, he spoke like one conscious of having done a noble deed.

'It isn't right yet, Tatham,' he declared, 'but there's stuff in it – don't worry. I wasn't going to refuse it because it wobbled a bit. I want to give it a chance. Some of it's A 1 – no kid! I can tell you what's wrong; *I'll* tell you what to do. I'm going to put my back into it for you.'

It appeared to be necessary to say that he was 'very kind'. Ross, with no ear for inflections this evening, deprecated gratitude. 'Not at all,' he murmured, 'not at all!' He produced the typescript – and it seemed to have aged years in his possession. 'Now,' he said, and objected to one of the best scenes; 'that won't do, of course.'

'You think not?' said Tatham blankly.

'Fatal, my boy! That wants to come bang out, and you've got to write something in its place. Turn it over in your mind, and –'

'Something in its place?'

'Well, I needn't have bothered you to come over if a cut was all that was necessary – *I* can *cut*,' replied Ross ingratiatingly; 'we want something written in there. Now here' – he licked his thumb and turned pages that revealed reckless scrawls, the burns of cigarettes, and splashes of tea or coffee — 'now here a cut will do the trick. This is in the way! All very carefully arranged, I know, but it's in the way. The audience don't want to hear *why* he wasn't drowned. Show him, my boy; it doesn't matter how he was saved, bring him on: 'That I am here to prove!' Terrific round of applause. See what I mean? You lose your grip if you explain things, Tatham. He's there! they know damn well he *has* been saved, because there he is! That's what we want in drama. And another thing –' Again he licked and turned.

It was strange: the author had thought his interest in the play was dead, yet it writhed under the scalpel.

'Another thing,' continued Ross, 'your villain isn't really a bad man, he only connives at a murder – you've got to strengthen your villain.'

'I tried to make him a human being.'

'We don't want human beings, my boy, we want parts. He shilly-shallies. That'll never do; he must be consistent, old chap; he mustn't have pangs of conscience. Why, you've given your villain lines that'd queer the whole show; the audience'd begin to be rather sorry for him! They don't want to be sorry for the villain, they want to hoot him. You'll have to alter that; you'll have to go over the part again and give him more relish for crime.'

'Oh,' said Tatham morosely. 'Is that all?'

'Well, I'm going to talk to you about my own part by-and-by – I want to get through the smaller matters first. You can't expect to do a drama without a little work, old chap, you know! Yes! this scene in the second act comes too soon, it wants transferring to the third – you'll have to turn the second and third acts about a bit to get it in, but it only needs a little thinking out. And there's a –'

'In other words, you want a different play?'

'What I want is a few changes,' replied Ross with heat. 'You don't mind making a few changes for the good of your piece, I suppose? I shall have enough to do on it when you're finished! A different play? Who said anything about a "different play"? I say that this one needs improving. So it does.'

'It needs rewriting, by what you tell me.'

'And precious few plays are submitted that don't!'

'Precious few plays are sold for ten pounds, though.' He forced a pleasanter tone. 'I've no doubt your criticisms are all perfectly right, but I can't afford the time. On the whole, I'd rather let the business slide.'

'What's the use of talking through your hat?' demurred Ross jocularly. But there was misgiving in his eyes.

'I'm quite serious. It doesn't amount to anything; I tell you frankly I'd never have done the thing if I had dreamed what you were going to offer for it. As to doing it over again, the mere thought of the job makes me feel sick.'

'Don't forget the kudos of a production, my boy – I take you into the Theatre!' He expatiated with much wealth of imaginative detail upon the glory that was included in his offer. 'And besides, a pound or two more or less needn't stand between us,' he added, noting that Tatham looked obstinate.

'Will you pay royalties?'

'Royalties?' echoed Ross. 'I never paid royalties in my life. I'll tell you what I'll do, I'll make it fifteen pounds, if you like. There!'

Now he was eager to secure the piece, and Tatham was far from eager to alter it. It was a situation in which the advantage was for once on the author's side. But he had gained the advantage by no subtler means than sheer weariness of spirit, and when the other repeated, 'Fifteen pounds. Come! And you can do all that's wanted in a week! he answered limply, 'Very well.' Had he been gifted with the foresight and ability to haggle with Ross for an hour, the actor would have agreed to pay a small royalty rather than see those four acts withdrawn from him – and Christopher Tatham would have been in possession of a comfortable income for many years.

The dilapidated typescript sprawled worthlessly on the couch. Even the expert who had been attracted by it would not have backed his fancy by a hundred pounds cash. To estimate the commercial value of a play before the production is as exact a science as to judge the potential value of a lottery ticket before the drawing – it may be a fortune, or wastepaper.

There were other interviews with Ross. He was not satisfied with the title that the author had chosen, nor was he satisfied with any of his own discovery. It was speedily evident that he expected Tatham to be as vitally interested by the matter as if they had been in partnership; and, to do the man justice, he was hospitable. There were long evenings passed in the society of Mr and Mrs Ross – an amiable and foolish little woman who, when the actor made her acquaintance, had been a fairy in a pantomime – during which a title was sought with an assiduity that entailed frequent refreshments. The host's consuming desire was to combine the words 'London' and 'Girl' in naming the drama – both, he declared, were 'lucky' – and one o'clock used to strike while the problem remained unsolved. Tatham's proposal, 'A London Girl' had been dismissed as much too tame for a playbill. Mrs Ross, simpering, had cried triumphantly, 'I know! "A Girl in London." It was the kind of suggestion that she usually contributed.

'What do you think of "Don't Let Your Girl Go to London"?' Ross inquired one night. Tatham said candidly what he thought, and Ross relapsed into gloom. 'Well, it amounts this,' he said, 'we can't have both! It's got be "London" or it's got to be "Girl".'

'I like "Girl",' chirped the lady.

'Yes, well, I like "London",' said her husband. 'Look here, Tatham, what the title's got to do is paint a picture of London as it – as it – to paint the whole blooming city. See what I mean? It's got to make the public think of London as it jolly well looks to a girl who's left her home and walks down the Strand, or wherever you like, without a penny in her pocket, asking herself what the devil she's to do for food and shelter. I want the public to stand looking at our bill in the High Street and thinking to themselves, "Ah me! Yes, indeed!" See what I mean? I want every young woman that reads the bill to put herself in the girl's place for a moment; I want every old woman that reads it to think of her own girl up in London. "Aye, and what about our Annie?" Then we've got their bobs – we pull 'em in to see the show that week! Do you like "Heartless London"? No – give us the cigars over here, Ruby! – no, that doesn't hit the spot. "A Lassie in London"? How do you like "A Lassie in London"?'

'She isn't a lassie,' said Tatham. 'What do you think of "A Girl Against the World"?'

Boss shook his head. 'I want "London"!'

'"London as it Really Is"?' said the ex-fairy.

'Rotten!' he growled. '"Yet London Laughs". Eh? "Yet London Laughs"! It's good?'

'What does it mean?' said Tatham.

'Mean? It means the heartlessness of London, of course! "Yet London Laughs"; in spite of everything – in spite of that poor girl's sufferings, London laughs!' He sighed. 'If you didn't see what it meant, it's off – a title's got to shout, or there's nothing in it. I want a title that's going to bring the wickedness of London before every pair of eyes in the provinces. I want to turn the West End, and the East End, and the whole bally caboodle inside out in three – I've got it!' A smile of beatitude overspread his face. 'Don't worry, my boy, don't worry; we needn't talk any more, I've got it! "London Inside Out".'

And to 'London Inside Out' he clung. Tatham made many attempts both on that evening and in their subsequent meetings to persuade him to change it – even going so far as to devise alternative titles as an inducement – but Ross was resolute. It mightn't be a 'literary' title, he admitted; as to that, he 'knew nothing and cared less; there was money in it, and money was what he was on the road for!'

It was not the sole source of argument. Peggy, fortunately, was again employed in another tour of *No Child to Call Her 'Mother'*, when the time came for his company to be formed; but Galbraith had appeared in Berners Street one Sunday morning, before the author was out of bed, to beseech him to 'use his influence' with Ross. Scrupulously shaved, and neat, but shabby with a shabbiness that was tragic, the suppliant sat at the foot of the bed, explaining that he had approached Ross vainly for an engagement, and confessing to despair. The danger of entrusting a part to him was so widely known that his chance of obtaining work grew slenderer yearly, and he unfolded a piteous tale of borrowed six-pences and destitution. Solemnly he swore that, this time, confidence in him shouldn't be misplaced. 'I've had my punishment, Tatham,' he faltered. 'If you knew all I've been through the last six weeks you wouldn't doubt me; there are things that nobody ever forgets. I– I slept in a registered lodging-house one night; another night, I slept on the Embankment. By God, boy, if you'll do what you can for me, I'll deserve it; I can't say any more.' His voice broke.

Not even in the urgency of his need did he hint, 'You owe it to me for introducing you to Ross!'

Tatham leant forward and gripped his hand. There were tears in the eyes of both men. 'I'll move heaven and earth for you, Galbraith,' he said; 'I'll go and see him this afternoon!' Much of the sum that had been paid for the play was in a pocket of the clothes that were heaped on the chair, and he thrust a five-pound note upon Galbraith. But the man wouldn't accept it; after much parley he consented to borrow a sovereign. They went out together for a steak at the Horseshoe; and when they had returned to Berners Street, Tatham left him in the bed-room with some cigarettes, and departed fervidly for Loughborough Road.

On the tedious journey his sense of eloquence abated somewhat. When he found strangers in the drawing room the additional delay reduced his confidence still more. Ross was plainly mystified by his arrival, for his visits at the 'residence', though frequent, had hitherto always been expected, and the embarrassment of intrusion weighted his tongue. He made perfunctory replies, but contributed no comments to the conversation, which was concerned with the iniquities of the 'bricks-and-mortar managers'. It was his earliest intimation that a 'bricks-and-mortar manager' signified the lessee of a theatre in which a touring company performed.

Presently he had a word apart with Ross, and they withdrew. 'Excuse me for a moment, boys,' said Ross, and led the way to the dining room. 'What is it, old chap?'

'Well, I'm awfully sorry to disturb you, but I've come to ask you to do something as a special favour to me,' began Tatham. 'Galbraith tells me you're afraid of engaging him. Now I've been with him all the morning; he's in frightfully low water, and I assure you he's to be trusted – I know what I'm talking about. You couldn't have a better man for "Colonel Forrester", he'd be excellent in the part. I want you to let him have it.'

'Not on your life!' said Ross. 'I know all about Galbraith. I know very well what he could do with the part – he's a jolly good actor; but I wouldn't have him as a gift.'

'Yes; well, I want you to reconsider your decision. He's a friend of mine. I've promised him to beg you to give him another chance. Now look here –'

'My dear chap,' interrupted Ross firmly, 'I'd do anything that I could to oblige you with pleasure, but –'

'You can do this!'

'But you're asking an impossibility! Galbraith? He's a pal of mine, too. I like old Galbraith very much – out of business; in it, I wouldn't have him at any price. It's no use, my boy! I gave him a chance when he was on his uppers; he took his sacred oath he'd keep his word if I tried him again. What happened? He was blind to the world on the first night in Bolton, before we'd been out three weeks! He means it right enough today; he's chock-full of good intentions while he talks, but he can't help himself; he's a madman – before the tour's half-way through it's the same thing all over again.'

'I've seen him touch nothing but water for months.'

'How many? Two's his record, ain't it? He'll be steady for a bit, I know, but he can't keep it up; all of a sudden he rolls on to the stage something horrible; it's a mystery to me how he manages to remember a word of his lines – if he hadn't been in the profession all his life, he'd be dumb, the state he gets in! I tell you straight, Tatham, I wouldn't have him if *he* paid *me*, I wouldn't have him if he offered a premium.'

They had not sat down; they were standing near the door, and he turned towards it with an air of finality. In his own interests, Tatham would have found no more to say, but in Galbraith's he wouldn't accept dismissal. The thought of the man's suspense in the bedroom, as the hours wore by, of his wretchedness if he must be told at last that the embassy had failed, spurred him to persistence in the face of defeat. He intercepted Ross, he spoke vehemently of its being a crisis in a mutual friend's life. Under the stress of feeling, rather unusual phrases came to his lips, and he was conscious and a little ashamed of sounding theatrical while he pleaded. Ross did not seem to be aware of it; he listened, frowning and restless, and there were signs of irresolution in his aspect now. Then Tatham stumbled on the word 'sentiment' and the actor was immediately defensive.

'No one's got more sentiment than me,' he cried. 'Sentiment? I'm the last man in the world to accuse of having no sentiment!'

'Well, listen to it today; don't be hard to a poor devil who's on the rocks! You'll be sorry if you are – you'll always be sorry afterwards. If I have to go back and tell him you refuse – well, Galbraith's desperate; on my honour, he's desperate! He's been sleeping on a bench on the Embankment. Suppose he makes away with himself tonight – more unlikely things have happened – how will you feel? A man you've been pals with for years?'

Ross blinked; his swimming eyes sought a highly-coloured oleograph on the wall.

'You'll always remember you could have prevented it! You'll never forget that a message from you today would have saved him, set him on his feet, given him a chance to turn over a new leaf!'

'It's a very unfair thing,' said Ross tremulously, 'for you to come and talk to me this way. Yes, it is, a damned unfair thing! – you aren't entitled to ask me to give him the part. *You* aren't risking anything; it won't cost *you* anything if he ruins the piece – it's my property, you've sold it right out.'

The advocate paused blankly. Then 'I know I'm not entitled,' he said. 'I'm asking it as a fine action, as a generosity; I'm appealing to your heart!' With a touch of inspiration, he added, 'to your sentiment!'

Ross gave in. He yielded reluctantly, but he yielded – and the gesture by which he proclaimed his unfailing sentiment's response was worthy of a large audience.

IV

With that incident the author's association with a melodrama from which every higher quality had been eliminated would practically have closed but for the gratitude of Galbraith. To attend the rehearsals, even had he wished to attend them, would have been impossible for a dramatist who sat every weekday driving a clerk's pen, and it was only by Galbraith that he was reminded of the play. Encouraged by his proximity to a salary, the 'Colonel Forrester' of the cast had succumbed to the offer of a further sovereign to supply immediate necessaries and improve his attire. An elderly figure in the frock-coat that had been released from the pawnbroker's, he presented himself in Berners Street on many evenings before the tour began; and it was he who wrote to Tatham after the opening night, announcing that the piece had 'gone like a house afire'.

To the man who had written the piece the news seemed extraordinary and well-nigh incredible. So far from rejoicing at it, since he had neither a pecuniary nor an artistic interest in its fate, his thoughts turned bitterly to the despised manuscripts, for which he had hoped and prayed. If it had been one of those that had 'gone like a house afire'? What it would have meant! Even if he had been such a consummate ass as to sell it for fifteen pounds, wouldn't he be rapturous, wouldn't he have trod Oxford Street tonight thanking God for the position that the success had given to him! There would have been reputation then, there would have been a future. This meant nothing – nothing but the satisfaction of Ross, who as yet had not written to express it, and the chance of perpetrating similar trash at better terms. He had done with trash. Never such fustian again!

The fools! A rush of disgust for the crowds whom it was delighting made him see red. He was unjust, he was unreasonable – he had planned his play for the majority, and they had welcomed it, he should have been grateful to them; but the artist who wept for two of his children in the corner drawer – just two, to be exact, the latest additions to the mortuary – could behold nothing but the irony of a very commonplace situation.

A very commonplace situation, indeed, in its essentials. But time emphasised it; the drawing power of *London Inside Out* proved to be conspicuous even among attractions of its class. From the reports of the correspondents of the theatrical organs, which Mrs Harper flourished at him when he paid duty visits, Tatham learnt only that the drama had been 'enthusiastically received' in the towns where it was performed; but a second letter from Galbraith apprised him that Ross was jubilant, and that there was every likelihood of the tour being extended much beyond the period foreseen.

In a narrative of humdrum humanity, let the reader be refreshed by an event that savours of the sensational and preposterous – Galbraith had enclosed a postal order for the two pounds; an unsuccessful actor had repaid a loan!

The author of an entertainment that was launched on a career of financial splendour in the provinces continued to contemplate the wall and the water-pipe, among other clerks, who had no suspicion of his achievement. At once ashamed of the work and of the price he had obtained for it, he spoke of it to no one, not even to his mother when at Easter he went to Sweetbay at a reduced fare and spent Sunday and much of Monday in the boarding house. Constitutionally incapable of keeping any secrets but her own, she would surely have announced the matter to his Regent's Park relatives, and he shrank from the thought of the questions that they all would ask him. He compromised with a sense of unfilial reticence by remarking that she stood in need of a new dress and giving her the money to have one made. The windfall elated her the more because the Spauldings had given her money for a dress the previous afternoon – arriving in their own car, when all the boarders were on the steps; and after he had gone she lost his present at bridge with a vivacious incapacity for the game.

No, he mentioned the play in no quarter, and when a few weeks had passed he did not hear of it any more, until a letter from Peggy revived the subject. The letter was headed 'Grand Theatre' and she wrote, '*London Inside Out* is against us at the Royal here and doing all the business. What ho! (Our houses are simply rotten.) I'm going to scramble tomorrow and get round in time to see a bit of it. One of our crowd met somebody in the show yesterday and heard that it is an enormous go everywhere. I say! if you had got royalties – what? Well, better luck next time, old boy! Naomi is joining our crowd. There was a fortnight's notice in the air, and I got wind of it, and gave her the tip. Won't it be jolly? This is a married crowd, pretty nearly, and I haven't made a pal in it.' She remained, with endearments, his Constant Sweetheart.

It was by far the most spontaneous letter that she had written to him for a very long time. The weekly correspondence strained her inventive faculties a great deal, for ordinarily there was nothing new to say, and she found it a most wearisome effort to cover a sheet of notepaper. She had arranged that when she was away she would write to him every Monday, but often her letter was dated 'Thursday' and even when Thursday had come and the necessity could be postponed no longer, she confronted it with very ill grace.

The posters of *London Inside Out* on the walls of the Lancashire town, however, had delighted her for more than one reason. Not only were they a promise of material for her letter this week, they made her more interesting in the eyes of her companions — she was engaged to the 'Christopher Tatham' whose name was to be detected in small type on the playbills. Of course, she had announced the name of her fiancé as soon as the piece was presented, exhibiting the notice in *The Stage* that announced its 'enthusiastic reception', but now her importance was driven home. The leading lady, whose amiability had hitherto had a touch of condescension in it, was calling her 'dear' quite warmly, and even old Miss Baker, who asserted that she had been with Barry Sullivan and was overbearing towards everybody else, grew cordial to her.

'I'm going to see a bit of *London Inside Out* tonight,' she told a young actor as they stood chatting in the wings. 'I wish they'd play up; ten minutes is about as much as I shall get of it, at this rate!'

'*I'm* going,' said Mr Nelson; his part concluded a few moments before her own; 'we'll go together, if you like. Don't take too long changing, though!' He was not one of the married members of the company to whom she had referred; he was a pleasant-faced boy not much older than herself, though, as an actor, he already told falsehoods about his age. 'They were chock-a-block there last night, eh?'

'Rather!' she said. 'All right, hang at the dressing-room door when you're ready. I shan't be long. I mean to get round before they finish, if I break my neck to do it.'

'I expect you'll see more of it than you want before long, eh?'

'Why, how do you mean?'

'The "best boy of all" will be getting you shopped in it soon, I suppose? Look at her conscious smile! What's the use of loving an author if he can't work engagements for us, eh? Yah, mercenary! You'll leave us for a better shop than this one, I bet!' He improvised, to an imaginary guitar:

> *Then she left us for a better shop than this one,*
> *Then she chucked the little crowd that loved her true;*
> *Though the tears were in our eyes,*
> *She forsook us for a rise,*
> *She departed for a difference in the screw!*

She thought how amusing he was. 'Silly idiot!' she laughed.

'I don't blame you! A faithful heart is broken, but what's a heart compared to £ s. d.? You girls were ever thus.

> *Then she left us for a better shop than this one –*

Is my hated rival very handsome, Peggy?'

'A jolly sight handsomer than you,' she chaffed back.

'Go on! If you'd met me first, he wouldn't have had a chance, not a glimmer. I can read your secret in your gaze – you struggle, Peggums. That's what you do, you struggle between love and lucre. Lucre cops the pool, but –'

'*You'll* cop a box on the ears if you don't look out,' she giggled.

'Your fair hand smite me, that little roseleaf?'

'The little rose-leaf can come down hard, I can tell you,' she said, enjoying herself.

She brought the palm of her hand in contact with his cheek, smartly enough to be a pretended blow, lightly enough to be a caress. His sprightliness appealed to her warmly; she regretted that, at the next instant, her cue was spoken. 'Hullo!' She darted. 'Bang – don't forget!'

It was five minutes to ten when she returned to the dressing-room and tore off her costume. She rubbed the cocoa-nut oil on her make-up,

84

and snatched at the grease-soaked rag, and plunged her face into the basin, exhilaratingly conscious that the other occupants of the room knew the explanation of her frantic haste. His knock was heard before she was ready, and somebody cried, 'There he is, let me hook you, dear!' with enthusiasm.

They sped down the alley, into Caledonia Road, in high spirits. Exchanging pleasantries in the darkness of the Market Square, her escort lunged at invisible opponents, and challenged her to race him to the pavement. It was much jollier than if she had been making the expedition alone.

'Nelson! behave yourself,' she laughed as they panted to the theatre steps. Then, at the box office, 'May we go in?' she asked hurriedly; 'we're at the Grand.' The delay while their cards were submitted to the local or the touring business manager – both gentlemen were in the buffet – was exasperating.

The last act was two-thirds over as the late-comers stole into the dress circle and descried vacant seats in a bad position, which were to be reached without disturbing anyone. The lights in the auditorium were lowered; but even so, she could see that the pit and pit-stalls were packed; and a few seconds later a burst of applause overhead informed her, by its volume, that the upper tiers were crowded too. She was deliciously proud of her engagement as Nelson nudged her, whispering, 'What a house!'

Her remembrance of the manuscript was too hazy for her to grasp the situation on the stage at once, but soon one of the characters exclaimed, 'The Colonel is coming back!' and she knew she was to see Galbraith. Vaguely she was conscious of a stir of discomposure among the people on her other side; almost at the same instant, an inarticulate but ironical greeting from the gallery struck her with dismay; and then Galbraith entered, treading the stage with slow uncertainty, the ponderous gait of an experienced actor fighting to conceal intoxication. He spoke, and she heard him dizzily, the words that he uttered reached her through a fog of horror, muffled, incoherent. Jeers from the gallery accompanied him. She held her breath, and perceived that the other actors on the stage were gagging, anticipating their cues, doing their utmost to accelerate the conclusion of his scene. Brief as it was, it seemed to her as if it would never end. The gallery approved his exit by shrill whistles.

'This comes of helping a pal!' she gasped. She turned to Nelson, trembling. Her face was colourless, it startled him. For an instant he had been almost as aghast as she, but his own consternation had yielded to amusement; he had failed to realise the fiancée's point of view. Now he strove to look sympathetically indignant, and patted her arm consolingly.

She was as furious as if she had been Ross himself; she quivered with a sense of personal injury. Mortified, she wished that Nelson had come in on the previous evening, or on the morrow; she had foreseen his returning to tell everyone how magnificently the show had gone, and, of all nights, Galbraith must select tonight to make a fiasco of it! So little attention could she pay to the rest of the act, that she was aware of nothing more than Ross's attitude as the curtain fell; and in the streets, during a walk that was very dull, she kept insisting, 'Of course, it was nothing to do with the piece, you know; they *ate* the piece – it was only Galbraith they were guying!'

For once she was impatient to write to Tatham. She wrote again on the following day and gave him such a highly-coloured account of Galbraith's condition that he wondered sadly how the fourth act of the play could have been reached at all. From the man he heard nothing; nor did he add to abasement by inquiries. But from the provincial columns of the theatrical paper at which he had the interest to glance, he learnt soon afterwards that an 'excellent rendition of "Colonel Forrester" was supplied by Mr Lionel Stott.'

The discharged actor did not reappear in Berners Street. Whether he was back in London, but too much ashamed to call, whether he was to be seen despairing in the professional haunts of Liverpool or Manchester, or whether the workhouse had hidden him, Tatham had no idea. On several Saturday afternoons he took his way to the Strand in the hope of information, but the neighbourhood revealed no more than one acquaintance – and he was relieved that their eyes did not meet. Elsie Lane was entering an agent's doorway. The quiet-voiced girl who a few years earlier had suggested a vicarage to his mind was painted like a harlot. The sight distressed him poignantly, the shock of it was in his mood all day, and for months the remembrance of the change in her moved his thoughts to sicker horror than the descent of Galbraith himself.

Meanwhile resident theatrical managers in the provinces awaited the arrival of *London Inside Out* with such keen financial interest that Logan Ross projected the formation of a second company to perform the piece, and urgent letters, marked 'Immediate, please forward,' reached Tatham from many actors and actresses with whom he had been associated formerly, and from many others of whom he had never before heard. They pleaded for engagements, and they appealed to him for loans. The clerk who had sold his play for fifteen pounds was entreated to 'extend a helping hand to less fortunate fellow-artists, now that he was a dramatist enjoying prosperity.'

V

On an autumn afternoon and the first day of his annual vacation, a city clerk descended from a third-class compartment to the platform of one of the last towns in the kingdom that any rational Londoner might have been expected to choose as the scene of a holiday. And as he strode from the station and viewed the utilitarian ugliness of the place, he beheld his boyhood too; and the spirit of a time that had seemed immeasurably behind and dead beyond the hope of resurrection came floating on the murky atmosphere to welcome him, lifting his spirit with a caress.

Which reveals to the mental eye that Christopher Tatham was not a rational Londoner, as 'rational Londoners' are estimated by the sound majority. There are moments, however, in which the possession of a temperament will yield delights unattainable by any bank balance. Ridiculous as it might be to derive emotions from a cobbled and very squalid High Street, and tall chimneys that belched black smoke into a dismal sky, this tripper was more moved by the prospect than if he had tripped for 'a week in Gay Ostend'.

In a shop window that he passed, a playbill of his drama was suspended, above mounds of margarine; on a hoarding, a crudely executed poster depicted a wildly sensational episode in the third act. The quotation from the drama, printed beneath the picture in striking capitals, was unfamiliar to him. What had brought him to the town? No affection for the piece, certainly, yet certainly a strong curiosity about it. Never had he witnessed a performance of this play, which, thanks to the expert's cuts and changes, had achieved such popularity that scores of struggling players imagined its author to be prosperous. For once he meant to see it. He didn't know that he was particularly wishful to see Ross; he was not sure that he would announce his presence to the gentleman. On the journey, his intention had been to pay for a low-priced seat this evening and to proceed to Sweetbay on the morrow – vaguely it was his intention still. But as he walked, he was increasingly aware of the past's embrace in the grim manufacturing spot whose like he had not trodden since a stage-door slammed behind him for the last time. Half deriding the idea, half yielding to it, he began in the neighbourhood of the margarine to ask himself whether he might not pass as many as three or four days of his holiday here.

His pace slackened. If he were, indeed, to remain for more than a night, the Black Bull would be too expensive for him, and he must seek a lodging-house instead. He felicitated himself that the bag he carried had been packed in ignorance of railway connections – his freedom was unfettered in a sufficiency of shirts. But he had no idea where the lodgings lay, and he remembered well that bags had a habit of developing weight while one explored. The Black Bull booked him after all.

It had been advertised as a 'Family and Commercial Hotel' but he saw only the commercials when he dined, and failed to enjoy their table manners. Practical men, these 'travellers' cast upon the unlovely scene by no caprice, and eager to do good business and be gone, yet Mr Tatham cavilled at their company. Partly it may have been – so poor is the texture of our reasons when examined! – because, in moments, he was conscious how widely they would grin at him, could they see into his sentimental mood.

If he had lingered for apple-and-blackberry tart, instead of rising so speedily for a stroll and a cigarette, his errant footsteps would not have brought him to the illuminated frontage of the Theatre Royal and Opera House within a few minutes of its doors opening; and if he had reached it some moments later than he did, Mr Logan Ross, who was exchanging financial opinions with the red-faced local business manager before proceeding to a dressing-room to don the immaculate flannels and 'wing' collar in which he leapt on to the stage from a punt, would not have started and halloed. As it was, the excursionist found himself shaking a large cordial hand, and trying to convey that his arrival in the town was quite unconnected with play-going, in fact purely fortuitous and unforeseen, almost before he realised what had happened.

Ross didn't write grateful letters, Ross didn't say, 'You're making a small fortune for me, God bless you!' but Ross was unfeignedly friendly in his greeting. He exclaimed that he had been wondering for months why the excursionist had 'never turned up' and presented him to the local business manager as 'my friend, Mr Tatham, the author of the piece.' And the local business manager said, 'Pleased to meet you, Mr Tatham,' with deference. The author of the most psychological play that ever deserved cultured encomiums and ran in the West End for a fortnight had never heard the note of respect that weighted the local business manager's salutation to the author of *London Inside Out*.

'You're coming in to see the show, Mr Tatham?' he asked, as one who craved a favour.

'Well, yes,' Tatham admitted, 'I did mean to.'

'He hasn't been near us since we've been out. What do you think of that?' said Ross. 'You can find a box for Mr Tatham, can't you, Fischer? Well, I must bolt, old chap! Come round afterwards; come round to my room. So long!'

Mr Fischer, with alacrity, found a box; Tatham sat in it in state. Every member of the cast threw a glance of curiosity towards it within two minutes of appearing on the stage; the eyes of every actor and actress sought his face surreptitiously throughout the evening, eager to divine his impressions.

And the piece went amazing: stupendous were the cheers and whistles. The fervid mass of operatives, small shopkeepers, mechanics, the rows of villa residents in the circle, where the ladies' attire approached the smartness of semi-evening dresses, were out for pleasure. No task of theirs to query whether such an 'accumulation of staggerers' could happen to any one hero in real life; they did not go to the theatre to remember real life – a strenuous or dreary affair at the best. Whole-heartedly they paid for theatre tickets to see life falsified, as Belgravia, and Bloomsbury, and Balham paid for theatre tickets – and library subscriptions – to see life falsified. More unsophisticated than Londoners, they were to be charmed by falsehoods more highly coloured; but, less self-conscious, they told no falsehoods to themselves – they did not seek to disguise their stolid indifference for all the arts by thinking they were art devotees because they enjoyed going to the play. And the gale of mirth when a fly-catcher stuck to the low comedian – a generous soul who kept pretending that he couldn't detach himself from it for as long as the last little girl in the pit would titter! And the storm of execration for the villain! And the appetite for refreshments – insatiable! 'A triumph for all concerned,' as the local *Advertiser* had stated in its criticism.

But *The Post*'s notice had yet to appear – and on the previous evening the 'triumph' had dejected *The Post*'s representative even more profoundly than most of the performances that it was her novel duty to attend when no one else on the staff was free to go. Very happily and proudly had she joined the staff a few months earlier; it was the first opportunity that she had found to earn a salary, though her pen had brought small cheques to her time and again. Very happily, too, had she learnt that it would sometimes be her task to 'do' the theatre. To write dramatic criticism – how interesting! It had been with a shock that she realised, instructed by a blue pencil and the powers, that locally 'dramatic criticism' meant indiscriminate praise. 'What use is that?' she had dared, dismayed. 'It's useful to the advertisement columns,' she was answered; 'it's what's expected. See?'

She had seen, and being a sensible young woman had done her best to obey. But dramatic criticism as practised on *The Post* had speedily ceased to be interesting to her. It became detestable; and though she was not aware of the fact, and though the editor-and-proprietor had as yet received no more than one complaint, the perfunctory praise had been diluted with so much truth that her feeble 'best' had aroused deep indignation in the mind of the manager of the Theatre Royal and Opera House. 'Whenever that girl came in, the show would be a blank sight better off without *The Post*'s notice!' he was wont to exclaim heatedly.

She was the eldest daughter of a parson in the country – a man who had a large family and a small living, and whose embarrassments with the tradespeople were not appreciably relieved by the manuscripts which, at long intervals, he dispatched to publishers in London. Compliments, but little pudding, they brought – those tributes to Nature, achieved in an overworked parson's scanty leisure; and the compliments were not uttered by his parishioners, who had barely heard of them, 'Squire' had received one and had acknowledged it politely, if late; but 'Squire' had received many circulars which interested him no less. Theodosia's thoughts had turned to her father's neglected books, to his lifetime of thankless struggle, as she beheld the Theatre Royal and Opera House rocked by enthusiasm for Mr Christopher Tatham's melodrama, and there had been bitterness in her heart for Mr Christopher Tatham. She had pictured him; and his jaunty self-satisfaction had incensed her more still. The moneyed cad of her imagination – her fancy portrait was, unconsciously, inspired by a shrinking horror of the red-faced business manager – had been contrasted with the figure of a scholar bowed over the 'study' table in a poverty-ridden home. Poor 'study'! When she was rich, Theodosia meant to endow it with an armchair that was comfortable, and a lamp that wasn't a curse, and a screen to keep the draught off that burdened back. It was not Miss Moore's function as a dramatic critic to think of furniture and lamps in a parsonage thirty miles from the low comedian and his fly-catcher; it was not discreet or fair of her to do it; but she was only twenty-four years old, and the evening was a crisis in her new career – the 'critic' had suppressed sincerity so long that suddenly it burst its dam.

She revolted. And after she went back to her lodging in King Street she wrote. She wrote a criticism that would never have been passed in the office of *The Post* if the editor-and-proprietor hadn't been in Blackpool, and the subordinate that reigned in his stead hadn't nodded on press night. When it was too late she found the criticism rather startling herself. Proprietorial displeasure looked to her very near at hand, for Mr Judd's absence was to be but brief.

Now, on the morning after Tatham's arrival in the town, some eight hours after he had parted from an elated and convivial Ross in that gentleman's 'diggings', he opened a nice clean copy of *The Post* in the 'smoke-room' of the Black Bull and was stung by what 'Footlights' had written. It stung him, not because 'Footlights' jeered at his 'dramatic triumph' but because 'Footlights' quite unwarrantably assumed him to be a successful person perpetrating similar trash habitually, and with complacence. (Here Theodosia's limited knowledge of the theatre had led her astray.) Thinking of the corner drawer again, he smarted to see himself referred to as the 'proud author of *London Inside Out*'.

Resentment was in his mind, and a supply of the hotel stationery stood alluringly beside him. He was still young enough to succumb to it. He wrote a sarcastic correction to 'Footlights'– too sarcastic, he was afraid, after the letter was posted. A rebuke in good humour might have been more effective. Indeed, as his temper subsided and he wandered among lodging-houses, seeking a couple of rooms neither too dear nor too dirty, he began to think that he might have committed a mistake in remonstrating at all. But he had no suspicion, of course, that he had made a second mistake in addressing his critic as 'Dear Sir'.

VI

Having now ascertained the names of the streets in which 'professionals' were offered a 'home from home, at moderate terms', he decided to avoid them, lest he stumbled on a house that sheltered a member or members of the *London Inside Out* company. He realised that he did not yearn to revert to the past in all its phases; he wished for selected features of the past. To linger in the wings once more for a few evenings would be pleasant enough; but since he had seen the performance, the chances of the low comedian or the villain proving congenial in the parlour looked to him remote.

People had praises to bestow on King Street, and to King Street he bent his steps. Cards in the miniature bay windows, on either side, announced 'Apartments' frequently, but brief interviews on doorsteps revealed always that this was a big name for a small bedroom. The general requirement of King Street appeared to be a young man engaged in business, and prepared to enjoy a tea-supper in the kitchen. However, at No. 43, he was recommended to try Mrs Leake's, the double-fronted house further up, and at Mrs Leake's his quest concluded.

Having been offered two little ground-floor rooms for less money than he paid for one at an inconvenient altitude in Berners Street, he hadn't done badly after all. He removed his portmanteau from the Black Bull, left his razor strop hanging on the curtain hook, ate a fried chop, and went to the theatre.

And at the theatre Theodosia had provoked excitement. He learnt it as soon as he entered Ross's dressing-room – learning primarily that Ross hadn't come to a malodorous hole like this to be taught the way to act. The statement was reiterated with a redundance of adjectives. It was manifest that, personally, Ross was more incensed by the impudence that dismissed his histrionic capabilities with mirth than by the diatribe upon the play; but he waxed informative by degrees – in front of a looking glass, while he smeared his face with the hues of youth.

'Jumped-up young idiot!' said Ross. 'How does the piece go – you were in last night, how does the piece go?' His narrative was delayed by expletives. 'Rotten amateurs getting two-pence a week on a thing that calls itself a "newspaper", trying to teach an experienced actor what to do with a part! Well, Picton's fed up with it – it isn't the first time – he's been round to the office and stopped his ad. "Accident be damned!" said Picton. "Think I advertise for the public to be told they're a pack of fools to come to the show? Not much!" said Picton. "Suppose I want to hear what your gory critic's opinion is? I don't give a rush for the gory opinion, one way or the other! What the critics are let in for is to do the show a bit of good, aren't they? If I pay for ads, I've the right to expect reciprocity, haven't I?"'

'That's one way of looking at it,' said the author.

'It's the *only way* of looking at it, my boy; the editor knew that very well – matter of business. Didn't attempt to defend himself, kept saying it was an 'error'. Picton behaved very well about it. As he said, if it had been a first offence he might have accepted the apology, but it wasn't; it's been going on for a long while, it was time for him to put his foot down... Do you see my moustache anywhere about? He wouldn't listen to any palaver at all – withdrew his ad then and there, quietly and firmly, like a gentleman. There's been a message sent round tonight: the girl's got the sack, and the editor says that the show shall have his hearty attention in the future; but Picton ain't going back on his word, and I don't blame him. Where the devil's the white hard varnish gone? I've been so upset over this thing all day – not for my own sake, for yours, my boy! – that, 'pon my word, I don't know what I'm doing.'

'What girl?' asked Tatham. 'Was it a girl, then?'

'Don't I keep telling you it was a girl? Judd, the boss, was away, I hear. Only got back this morning, and was in a blue funk before Picton went in; he knew he'd lost an ad as soon as he saw his blessed rag today. "Tearing passion to tatters" me? That's what I made my reputation on, eh? If there's a thing I do pride myself on, it's my restraint. They didn't half like me at the Rotunda, did they? I didn't get a return date in Leicester simply and solely, I pledge you my word, on the artistic merit of my own performance! "Tearing passion to tatters"? It's too silly to talk about.'

While he continued to talk about it, and it was the staple subject of his discourse throughout the evening, it was apparent that the journalist's dismissal was a point that had made absolutely no impression on his mind. On the business manager's and Mr Picton's it was impressed,

Tatham perceived later – they spoke of it with lively satisfaction; but, fluently as Ross discussed the criticism, when all but the buffet lights were out, and glass succeeded glass, the critic's loss of her berth was a feature of the affair upon which he had no remark to make. He was not heartless, he would have put his name to almost any subscription list that was brought to him, and – as he hadn't failed to remind Tatham – he had compassionately, and against his better judgment, engaged Galbraith. But he was an actor. Passing his life in the most precarious calling in the world, among men and women who seldom dared to expect to retain any engagement for a longer period than three or four months, a girl's loss of employment seemed to him as commonplace as a wet day. He was honestly surprised at Tatham's reference to it, when they left the theatre together.

'I daresay she'll soon get shopped somewhere else,' he said. 'You don't mean to say you're worrying about that?'

'It's a serious thing getting the sack; I know what it means.' He wished that he hadn't written to her, wondered if she held him partly responsible for what had happened.

'Well, we all know what it means!'

'It's not the same thing to lose a temporary engagement as to lose a permanent job. Perhaps she expected to remain on the paper for years... And, after all, a great deal of what she said was true; I'm not talking about the acting – what she said of the piece. We know what the piece is, ourselves.'

'Piece is a property, old man,' said Ross, who was in much better spirits since the dalliance in the buffet. 'And it's going to be a bigger boom still, it's going to be a money-maker for years to come. If you can only keep the game up, you'll be all right. Look here, if anybody wants to know your terms for another piece as good, you ask *me*! Don't sell your next piece for fifteen quid, Tatham. Come to *me*, *I'll* give you the tip. Your name's known today, my boy – they're asking about you in the provinces.' He added diplomatically, 'Of course, they don't know how much work *I* put in on the scrip!'

Tatham unbosomed himself. 'I loathe the muck. I wouldn't write another thing like it unless I were starving. Besides, I don't think I could! ... I'm working for London.'

They proceeded in silence for a few moments.

'Between you and I, perhaps you're right,' Ross admitted. 'It doesn't matter about it's being "muck" – if the public don't know any better, why should we care? But *I'm* not sure it's in you to do the trick again, either; you might strike a plot, but you'd go all wrong in the way you worked it. And, of course, a good half of the success of this is due to my performance – the part suits me. Yes, I should say lighter stuff for the West End would be more in your line – if you can get your foot in. I don't know that this is going to help you, though.'

Tatham turned a slow stare upon him. 'What do you mean? Do you mean it's going to hinder me?'

'Well, the West End managements have heard of it – don't make any mistake about that; and they're going to hear of it more still, I promise you! They're precious sidey in the West End, old chap – sneer their important heads off at this sort of show, though they're often sick with envy to think of the business it's doing. I shouldn't wonder if they weren't particularly keen on reading a play by the author of *London Inside Out*; they may think you aren't class enough for their high-and-mighty houses. Still, you'll see; it's only an idea – very likely, I'm wrong... Coming in for a nightcap?'

No, he wasn't going in tonight. He strolled on to King Street, wondering what foundation there might be for the idea, and saw too late that the wiser course would have been for him to write the melodrama under a pseudonym. But who could have conjectured that the thing was to become so widely known? 'The proud author of it' he had been called this morning; tonight he was told that it might stand in his way as long as he lived. Again he remembered his retort to the girl, and while he supped kept wishing that his note had not gone. Of course, she was including him among the forces that had made for her calamity – at any rate she assumed that he had grinned to learn of it! They were never likely to meet; she moved through his fancy as a spectacled little frump; but it chagrined him to reflect that somewhere in the world, till they both were laid to rest, there was to be a spectacled little frump who thought meanly of him... To write again and express his regret for what had happened? That might be to make a second blunder!

Miss Moore was, indeed, thinking meanly of him no further away than the sitting-room over his head. And the lady also repented of sarcasm – scribbled in answer to his own before she had been discharged. She had not foreseen a reproof so summary as that, or she would have answered nothing. Now she reflected that the man would jeer at her reply, since doubtless her punishment was known at the theatre; he would jeer and could afford to jeer at it. For the thousandth time she wished she had restrained that impulse to repartee. Then for the thousandth time she tried to banish Mr Christopher Tatham, and Mr Picton, and Mr Judd from her mind and asked herself what she was to do.

Go home? She had no reproach to fear there, they would be tenderness itself. She saw her father's half-humorous smile, felt his arm about her waist; she heard the girls' chorus of sympathy and indignation; she would not be humiliated in confessing to that group what a fool she had been. But as she sat gazing at the shavings in the lodging-house grate, Theodosia looked beyond the arrival and the chorus – viewed the straitened circumstances and the extra mouth to feed; she beheld herself waiting, from week to week once more, for a guinea cheque which was so sorely needed to appease the butcher and which a London editor took so long to write. No, she couldn't go home – she had to keep herself!

Somebody, a new lodger downstairs, jarred the silence by knocking the ashes from his pipe into the fender.

'Keep myself!' muttered Theodosia, nodding to the shavings.

How? There was no chance on *The Advertiser*, she was sure of that. It meant London, then! If she didn't go home, she must go to London and try to find employment on one of the few papers that had taken her short stories. The most recent and the most literary of them dominated her reverie. From the Editor of *The Aspect* she had twice received an encouraging, even a flattering letter since she had been on *The Post*. What if she presented herself at the office of *The Aspect* and explained her necessities to her kindly correspondent? Surely, since her tales had interested him so much, he would consent to give her something to do regularly? She might – she could – Mentally she turned the leaves of *The Aspect* and asked herself just what columns of the journal, apart from the story, she was competent to write. The question found no answer, nor was she sanguine of the ability to produce even a short story every week; but memory echoed the dulcet phrases of the gracious letters, and she felt that an editor who had addressed her in so benign a fashion would prove a friend.

She had never stayed in London. She had seen Westminster Abbey, and St Paul's, and the National Gallery, and the British Museum, and had often asserted glibly that she 'knew London', but all at once her knowledge of it shrank and left her startled. The city loomed before her very vast and strange. She realised that she would find no bedroom in the buildings that she had visited, and that she had no idea to what quarter to direct the cabman when she reached the noisy station. Her father's arm and her sisters' welcome looked sweetly restful; the shavings grew misty before her eyes.

She was crying, how ridiculous of her! She rose impatiently, and was surprised by the tidings of the clock. Well, she could breakfast as late as she liked – there was no desk to go to now. Those people, those horrible people, and the cad who had written the preposterous piece! One day, when she had got on, she'd look back and laugh at all their petty spite!

'Oh, I *am* so miserable!' she quavered to the silence.

At war with the world, the new lodger downstairs clattered his pipe furiously again.

VII

It was not till the morning, when he couldn't shave in comfort, that he missed the razor strop, hanging to the Black Bull curtain-hook. After breakfast he went to fetch it; and among the bottles in the bar there was a note for him. The loftiness of its tone was less exasperating because he divined the depression of the writer, but it irritated him enough for him to read the note twice. It was in reading it for the second time that he noticed the address at the top and learnt that 'T. Moore' was living in the same house as himself.

To defend himself, to express his sympathy, or to see what she was like? He could not have said precisely why the discovery inspired him with the wish to call upon her, but it did not seem an unnatural thing to do, since they were sheltered by the same roof; he could not think that she herself would consider it unnatural in the circumstances. To his own mind it seemed more unnatural that they should be writing to each other, with only a ceiling between them.

The householder was washing the doorstep when he reached it and inquired if 'Miss Moore' was at home. 'Will you tell her I should be very grateful if she would see me, please?' Mrs Leake, surprised but docile, went upstairs drying her hands, and reappeared to tell him that 'Miss Moore was in the drawing room.' He knocked, and was bidden to 'come in'.

She looked very tall against the miniature mantelpiece. She was standing, her back to the shavings, a little curiosity and a glimmer of amusement in her eyes. His own widened as they met her face, and as the frump of his fancy fled and left him startled, he wondered a shade breathlessly what he had come to say.

'Miss Moore?' He fumbled with his hat and cane on the threshold. 'I must apologise for my visit, I've just received your letter. I wanted to tell you that I was exceedingly sorry for mine.'

'Won't you sit down?'

'Thank you. I – fear I was rather brusque – stupid; of course, it was your business to say just what you felt about the play. Only a man isn't necessarily "proud" of what he has written.'

'Nor a woman,' she said, with the suspicion of a smile.

There was a pause. He looked away from her, and back again, and blurted, 'I hope you don't think *I* had anything to do with the complaint that was made to the Editor?'

'I was told it was Mr Picton who had complained,' she said evasively. The chill indifference of her tone lent him no aid. It was with an effort he repeated:

'But I hope you don't think I had anything to do with it? I knew nothing about it till it was over. Not that I could have prevented it, anyhow, but I shouldn't like you to confuse the author with the Management. You aren't blaming *me*?'

'I've no right to blame anyone – unless it's myself. I wrote what I really thought about the piece. That was unwise. It really isn't in the least necessary to talk about it.'

'I hope you'll pardon my intrusion,' said Tatham, as formally as she.

'Oh, it was very kind of you to call.'

'I was fool enough to write to you, but I wasn't cad enough to wish to do you any harm. And I was frightfully sorry when I heard what had happened. There's nothing else.' He got up. 'I must thank you for receiving me, Miss Moore.'

She regarded him steadily for a moment; her face softened.

'I *really* think it was kind of you to call, Mr Tatham,' she said, putting out her hand.

'Ah!' he exclaimed; 'you do believe me, don't you? If I had any voice in the matter, you'd be back on the paper this afternoon.'

'You're very magnanimous,' she smiled. 'I'm afraid – it's a humiliating confession – I'm afraid my criticism was rather vulgar?'

'Not that. But rather – may I say it?'

'I mustn't object to candour.'

'Rather unfair, then. You hated the play – I'm not surprised – but wasn't it a little unfair to take it for granted that I thought it a masterpiece, myself?'

'I don't think I said that, did I?'

'That I was "proud" of it, that I couldn't do anything better?'

'Oh, I thought you could do better. There were things here and there that made me think you could do ever so much better, if you cared to. That was why I – I wondered.'

'Looked down on me, you mean?'

She sought for euphemisms. 'That was why I wondered how you could be content to write that.'

'I wrote "that" for the same reason that you wrote criticisms of the theatre. The work didn't interest you very much, I imagine – the plays that come here tax your patience more than your intellect, don't they? From my own point of view, I have to live.'

'Ah!' She seemed about to annihilate him, but checked the retort. 'You won't tempt me to accuse you again!'

'Accuse?'

'I could answer what you've said.'

'Go on!'

'Shall I? Well, people may manage to "live" without stooping to quite such profitable work as you do.'

'What is it?'

'Oh, please don't ignore the "triumph"!'

'And the rest?'

'I suppose you *have* written other pieces, and will write more?'

'I hope so. But none of the others has ever been produced — and none of them made me feel ashamed when I wrote it.'

Again they looked at each other in silence.

'I've jumped to conclusions?' inquired the girl.

'Frantically, since you ask the question. You seem to think that one swallow makes a summer – you seem to think that if a piece is a success, the author must be rolling in money. It wouldn't do me any good if *London Inside Out* ran for generations.'

After absorbing this, she murmured, 'I'm sorry I wrote in the way I did.' And added drily, 'You're nobly avenged.'

'Is it impertinence to ask whether –' He hesitated.

'Whether there's any other paper waiting for me? No, Mr Tatham, there isn't. *The Post* appointment was the first I've had.'

'It's a cowardly shame,' he cried. 'If I were anybody I'd go and talk to the man. But it isn't what you said about me he minds; of course; it's the loss of the advertisements. Well… what are you going to do?'

'I suppose I'm going to look for something else,' she fenced.

'Here?'

'Oh no, there's nothing in this place. I – I daresay I shall go to London.'

'Have you — is there any prospect there?'

'Oh, I'm not afraid of the experiment. Please don't take it so seriously; very likely I might have had to leave *The Post* soon, in any case – one never knows. It was awfully nice of you to come to see me – I didn't deserve it.'

There was finality in her tone. He regretted, but accepted the dismissal. 'Well, goodbye, Miss Moore.'

'Goodbye,' she said. 'And thank you again… I'm afraid it'd be no use for me to ring, the landlady wouldn't understand what it was for.'

'Oh, I'm not going away,' he explained. 'I live here.'

'Here?' She was very much surprised. 'In this house, do you mean? Are *you* the downstairs –'

'Yes,' he said; 'I'm the "downstairs". I hope I haven't disturbed you?'

'Oh, not in the least,' she said hurriedly; 'no. I heard you knocking out your pipe, that's all – it was your pipe, wasn't it? But I thought you were at the Black Bull?'

'For a night. Yes, it was my pipe; I'll take care this evening. I'm in the town for three or four days – it wouldn't run to an hotel for so long as that. I'm a very much less opulent person than you fancied, not nearly so professional as yourself. I'm a clerk – this is my holiday.'

Now if he had announced that he was a wealthy amateur, Theodosia would have bowed again and the interview would have ended; but because he was revealed as a humble clerk she felt more remorseful still for her derision of him in *The Post*; and instead of letting him go, she smiled the sunniest smile that she had given to him yet and said, '*Are* you? If the world's so ungenerous to us both, we ought to be friends. Oh, I do wish I hadn't been so horrid about you! Where do you live? In London? Perhaps you can tell me something I want to know?'

And, instead of having descended to the parlour a minute later, he was sitting down again in the drawing room and digesting the fact that she proposed to adventure London, equipped with hope, a pen, and little cash. The intelligence was imparted so casually – his advice, obviously, being sought on no weightier matter than the localities of cheap furnished apartments – that the counsel in his mind was not easy to utter. He felt constrained, though, to urge that pens were more numerous than salaries in London, and that to Fleet Street her experience on Mr Judd's organ would prove no Open Sesame.

'I hate to depress you,' he said, 'but if you'll let me speak plainly, I think it would be a far better plan for you to write to the editors who know you. If they can offer you anything, they can tell you so by letter – you needn't travel to disappointments, you can find them with a penny stamp. Of course, I've no right to interfere –'

'Oh, you aren't interfering!' she exclaimed petulantly. But he felt that she repented her confidence. And she was, in truth, uncomfortably conscious of having blundered into a position of little dignity. 'I've no doubt you're perfectly right; what you say sounds very practical.'

'Why are you wishing you hadn't told me?' asked Tatham impulsively.

'What?' It was spontaneous, the quick surprise of a woman responsive to a man's intuition. 'Was I? Oh, I don't know. I suppose I was wondering why on earth I should have bothered you about it!'

He shook his head. 'You were thinking you had paid me too great a compliment. I was afraid you might! If I had been insincerely sanguine, you'd have liked me much better.'

'You're calling me a horribly ungrateful person! So' – she forced a laugh and turned to him – 'you think the idea's very silly, do you? The advice you give me is to put my pride in my pocket and go back, beaten – to confess I'm a failure? Think before you speak! – I mayn't forgive you a second time.'

'I think you'd do much better to go home if you've no prospects and no friends in London,' said Tatham obdurately. 'Yes.'

The moment in which her eyes dwelt on him seemed a very long one.

'Well, I haven't told you quite everything; I *must* find some work to do in London,' she declared. But there was no lack of forgiveness in her voice, there was frank approval. 'I'm much obliged to you for not being insincerely sanguine, all the same.'

'Very well,' said the man, 'that point's settled. Now let's consider where you're to live! Don't you know London at all?'

'I've often been there for a day. That doesn't count, I'm afraid. Is Chelsea far away? I've always thought I should like to live in Chelsea; it's such a pretty name, and there's the river.'

'I don't exactly know how you get to Chelsea,' said the Londoner vaguely. 'Yes, I think it is a long way off. If you're going to call on editors, you'd find the West Central district more convenient, I should think; you'd be able to walk to where you want to go… I suppose you want two rooms, don't you?'

'Well, yes, I certainly do,' said she, 'if I can afford the price. Why? Are they going to be dear?'

'They're going to be much dearer than two rooms here. Where I am, I've only one. Do you know, I think a boarding-house might be the thing for you. It would give you a sitting room – or a corner of a sitting room – and it'd save you an awful lot of trouble about your meals; you'd have no things to order and you wouldn't be cheated.'

'Oh, that's a capital idea,' exclaimed Theodosia brightly. 'You're being tremendously useful, Mr Tatham. Go on! Where am I to find a boarding-house, a nice cheap one, near the paper offices?'

'Well, I don't know the address of any paper,' he laughed, 'except the theatrical papers, but I expect the West Central district is about as nice and near as you'll be able to get. You can see any number of them advertised in the *Telegraph*. I'll bring a copy in. You'll see the terms too, and you can pick out something likely and arrange ahead by letter. How soon do you mean to go?'

'I meant to go tomorrow; I don't want to waste time. My fortune's limited – the longer I wait before I go, the less there'll be of it when I get there.'

'I should wait for an answer,' he insisted. 'If you arrived and found the house full and had to drive about with your luggage on the cab, looking for a place to live in, it'd be a miserable day for you. It wouldn't do at all; there are all sorts of objections to it – your people ought to know where you'll be. I'll go and get the *Telegraph* at once – I daresay I can get it at the station – and I'll mark the suitable addresses for you. Shall I?'

'You're most awfully good,' said Theodosia gaily. 'It'd be lovely of you.'

VIII

So in the afternoon he tapped at the door again, and he was aware, in betaking himself to the wings later, that his day had passed with unusual swiftness. On his return he entered the passage lightly, and when he banged his pipe on his palm, instead of on the fender, he fell to wondering what London might have in store for the girl overhead.

Also he wondered a little at the music of homely English words, now that he had heard a gentlewoman's voice again. How different was every vowel of her vocabulary from the vowels of the group he had just left! She spoke another language – the language that Ross made a horrible attempt to speak as the hero, in the moments when he remembered that he was supposed to be well-bred and said, 'It's naice of you, I'm shoeah!'

Great mistake for her to go to London – she couldn't afford to stay there long enough to do any good! Not of vital importance, though, as she had people to write to – she needn't starve when she had spent her money. Still, she was bound to find town very sad and lonely: he caught himself wishing that he had a married sister to look after her. What, in heaven's name, was it to do with him? London was full of lonely girls clamouring for work – they were dragging their feet up and down the agents' stairs all day. Not girls like her! thought she was so different from – Again it reverted to that – she was 'so different'! The image of Peggy obtruded itself violently. The dishonesties of the mind are innumerable: subconsciously he had striven to exclude Peggy from his reflections; he had sought to keep Peggy out of sight for Peggy's own sake; he felt queerly guilty and compassionate towards Peggy as her shortcomings thrust themselves into a fatal comparison. He reminded himself conscientiously that his appreciation of Miss Moore was purely intellectual.

The next morning moved more slowly than its predecessor, and Mrs Leake, who brought no enlivening message, was a disappointment to him every time she entered the room. To Theodosia, too, the hours were long. She divined that the rain looked no less dismal from the dining-room window than from her own, and knew that she would find it pleasant to talk to him; but she was a foreigner in bohemia, and, for once, doubtful of the social laws of the land she knew. She was diffident of inviting the man to 'come upstairs' and equally afraid of seeming thankless. Yesterday she had called a stranger her 'friend' and today she was ignoring his existence. Did works on etiquette by members of the aristocracy provide for this situation? She determined it in the early afternoon, without the aid of those invaluable manuals, by inquiring through the landlady if he would come up to tea at five o'clock.

And on the following day the second post brought a satisfactory letter, which civility required her to display.

'I've heard from the house in Torrington Square,' she informed him; 'there'll be a small room free tomorrow, so I shall go from here in the morning. She wants me to let her have a postcard to say whether I'm coming, or not. You go tomorrow too, don't you, to Sweetbay?'

'Yes. I go all the way to London first, though,' he said. 'I've been asking at the station – it'll be much quicker. We might go by the same train, mightn't we? – then I can look after your luggage for you when you arrive.'

Why not? She admitted frankly that it would be much pleasanter than travelling by herself. And, by-and-by, when she went to the pillar-box, they met again in the streets. The sun was shining, and after the postcard was dispatched they walked together, past the factories, along a white road that wound between hedges to the unknown. During their walk they learnt a good deal of each other; and more than once Tatham asked himself whether it would be the right thing to mention that he was engaged. His mind recoiled from mentioning it, primarily because it seemed to him that it would be as if he said, 'You must never aspire to marry me, you know; I should be sorry for you to have any false hopes – let me warn you not to expect it!' Wasn't she bound to realise the reason that he told her? wouldn't he deserve to be most disdainfully snubbed? But also he was deterred by the dread of having to dilate upon the subject of Peggy to her, doubting his ability to sound as enthusiastic as he ought. He talked instead of his failures and his ambitions. She was not bored by the story of his failures; a passing reference to the corner drawer hadn't sufficed for her, and her interest was so vivid that they had turned back from a neighbouring village and were half-way home before the drawer was shut. Nor was it only the girl who had questions to ask; he was granted a view of the 'study' and obtained surprising glimpses of the Church as a profession.

'I should like to read some of your father's books,' he said. 'And your stories – are they always signed?'

'Generally. *The Aspect* cuts me down to initials, though – "T. M.". T stands for "Theodosia"; perhaps that's why they won't print my name in full, it takes up such a lot of room. I'll send one to you one day, when I've done something I'm particularly vain of.' She laughed. 'Then you can avenge yourself; you can call me "the proud author of a silly little story". Isn't it funny, if I hadn't written that –'

'Yes, I know, I've been thinking of it! If you hadn't written that, I should never have spoken to you… I suppose I might have seen you through the window when you went out – wondered who you were!'

'And you'd have gone on clattering your pipe in comfort and have had nobody's luggage to bother about tomorrow but your own. I'm wondering so hard what he's like.'

He didn't say 'Who?' In looking back, she gave him credit for that.

'He'll be very polite,' he prophesied, 'if he's written to you so nicely. But –'

'No, don't! You were quite discouraging enough the day before yesterday.'

'I talked as I should have talked if you'd been my sister.' Again he wished that he had a sister, married, capable, urbane.

'I know. Oh, I know it'll be extraordinary if anything comes of it! But –'

'I don't think it'd be extraordinary if you found an opening in time, but I don't see *The Aspect* ready to take you on the staff the moment you suggest it. I daresay he'll be polite enough, but I'm afraid you'll walk back to Torrington Square in the blues.'

'There are more papers than one in London. Everybody has to begin. How do other people get on?'

'I can't tell you,' said Tatham; 'I haven't done it.'

'Haven't other women like me gone there and managed to stay? Anyhow, I'm not going to give in till I'm forced to – I've got to do my best first. Think of me besieging editors when you're listening to the band on the pier!'

He was conscious that he would; hazily, too, he was conscious that the interest afforded by his trip had been a surprising interest, and that, in retrospect, the theatre would be a less vivid impression to him than this walk along a country road. Actually, what he was to recall most often was the confusion at the terminus next day and her troubled face through the cab window. So capricious is memory, which immortalises moments without reference to our tastes and expectations!

The journey had been well enough, but at the last there was difficulty about her luggage after all. The porter who went to fetch it was absent so long that Tatham left her and went to look for him, and when the man was found, he had mumbled that the trunk was missing. It was discovered at the other end of the platform, after the other passengers had all departed. Her smile of relief was radiant, but the minutes in which it had appeared that her belongings might be anywhere excepting in the van had taken the colour from her cheeks.

'Well, I'm all right now! Ever so many thanks for everything, Mr Tatham. I hope you'll enjoy yourself at Sweetbay.'

'Thanks. *I* hope – well, you know!'

'Though I've defied your advice!' This afternoon her laugh was a little nervous.

'I feel much more sanguine this afternoon, somehow,' he affirmed untruthfully; 'I've an idea my advice'll turn out to have been wrong. Then I'm to hear your news when I come back next week?' The cab was moving, he kept pace with it eagerly. 'If you do change your address before then –'

'I shan't,' she said, 'before next week!'

And as the gates were passed and she looked out at London, she felt less lonely for the thought that next week she was to see him.

IX

If she had written a story about them both – and though she didn't do it, she had half a mind to write a story beginning, 'The dramatic critic of an obscure newspaper sat in the dress-circle' – nothing would have been simpler than for untoward circumstances to prevent their meeting again for years: the boarding-house might have proved impossible, even for the briefest of sojourns, and he might have been told when he called there that she had gone without leaving any message. In reality, no such dramatic complications occurred. The dinner was deplorable, and the boarders were depressing, and the artificial cheerfulness of the propri-etress was melancholy beyond words, until she gave the effort up and lapsed into contemplation of her liabilities; but having expected nothing better for the money, Theodosia remained.

She remained, and when she had heard, with a sinking of the heart, that her encouraging correspondent of *The Aspect* was out of town, and not due at the office for a week, her days were devoted to attempts to see the other editors who had published her work.

At the outset she saw no further than a printed interrogation form presented disconcertingly by a liveried official at the entrance. The form demanded terse statements of all that she mistrusted her ability to urge at length. It was displayed to her by Thursday that these imperative de-mands for information were finding her too docile. After she had acknow-ledged her insignificance several times with discouraging results, she began to palter with the peremptory inquiry, 'Business?' She euphemised, she grew disingenuous. Once she had the audacity to ignore the inquiry altogether, and discovered that the alarming official regarded his duty as accomplished when he had indicated the form to her, caring not a row of his domestic pins whether she complied with all its requirements or not.

Theodosia's earliest impression of her London editors when she had stormed their thresholds was that they were unaffected and rather chatty gentlemen who appeared incapable of declining desirable manuscripts with the dilatory tastelessness of which she knew them to be guilty. It was, for instance, sensational to remember that the meek-mannered little man who tittered to her in the office of *Mother and Girls* was the remorseless power who had rejected every story that she had offered to him during six months. So sweetly, even persuasively, did he suggest her 'letting him see some more of her stories' that it seemed – until she sent one – as if she were destined to delight him by everything she wrote. But when she explained that she wanted some regular work, he 'feared'. She had often reflected that she could make the columns signed 'Lady Fervia' very much more interesting than 'Lady Fervia' contrived to do, and only her reluctance to disparage another woman's work prevented her asking the little Editor if he was satisfied with them. When he inquired with a simper, 'And how do you like Lady Fervia's stuff? – I do that myself,' she was glad she had refrained.

Then there was the gentleman who explained that his periodical was an object lesson to all the other editors in London – she was not sure but what he included those in America. And there was the Editor who talked enthusiastically of 'literature' and bewailed the ignorance of the class of readers for whom he was condemned to cater. He favoured her with examples of his literary tastes – pearls from deep thoughts – and, although she was a nobody, she knew that their polysyllabic pretentiousness wasn't quite so admirable as he thought it was. And there was the good-natured, paternal Editor who counselled her candidly to return to the country.

A good deal of her time was spent in waiting rooms, and she found it fascinating to try to guess the business of the other occupants. The black-and-white artists proclaimed their purpose by the sketches that they nursed; but she used to wonder which of the disconsolate-looking company were the story writers, and if they were professionals or amateurs, and what their fate was to be when their turn was announced at last. Sometimes, as she watched them, they became the heroes and heroines of embryonic stories themselves, and it was a regret to her that, after they hurried from their seats at the summons of a swooping boy, who passed his life flying up and down the stairs, she didn't see them any more, and was left with her little romance unfinished.

One afternoon she had a conversation in a waiting room. She had sighed, 'It's tedious, isn't it?' and the woman had answered, 'Well, *I'm* glad of a chance to sit down!' She was dressed much more expensively than Theodosia, and the girl, who had assumed her to be successful, was rather surprised by the sadness of her tone.

'Are you working for the paper?' asked the woman.

'No.' With a vague idea of justifying her presence, she added, 'I had a tale in it some time ago.'

'Oh, fiction!' She sounded envious and inimical. 'Yes, that's the best – if one can do it.'

'Do you think so?' It was an arresting point of view.

'Anything that one can do at home!'

'It doesn't mean a salary, though – one gets a story taken now and then.'

The sad woman was inclined to envy and dislike her less. 'Have you been writing long?'

'I haven't been making a living by it very long.'

Both smiled.

'It's a beastly business,' said the woman. 'I haven't been at it long, either; it's the first time I've been on a paper. I'm doing the fashion article.'

'Is that the easiest sort of work to find?' asked Theodosia eagerly. 'I do so want to get something permanent.'

'I'd advise you to do anything else instead.'

'It's so tiring?'

'Oh, it's tiring, of course – I've been running about the West End all day; it's the same thing every day; and when I get home, dead beat, in the evening I've got to write. But it isn't only that it's tiring! If your name isn't well known, you can't keep yourself just by writing the articles – there aren't half a dozen women in London who get big enough terms for their stuff to do that – you've got to canvass for advertisements besides. It isn't very pleasant.'

'No, I don't think I should like that,' said Theodosia.

'I don't think you would! – especially if you were doing it for a rag like this. I daresay it's all right if the paper has a large circulation, and the shops know it; but when I go in and say I'm representing a paper they've hardly heard of, it's as much as they'll do, very often, to let me see their models. When I try to persuade them to pay for advertisements –'

'It must be loathsome!'

'One's got to live,' sighed the other. 'But don't try canvassing if you can manage any other way. It's worse still for a girl – I've a friend who used to do it.'

'Why "worse"?'

'Because it's men you have to see. At Madame Diane's you see Mrs Brown, but at Clifford's, or Lacy and Lovell's, or any of those places, it's always a cad of a man you've got to talk to. You can imagine what it means. He says, "I'm not sure if I can give you an ad, but I'll take you out to lunch if you like!"'

An indefatigable boy, swooping like his counterparts elsewhere, interrupted them before her confidences could be continued. But when a well-intentioned editor, who had not heard such confidences, offered the girl an opportunity to devote her energies to the advertisement columns of a struggling periodical, it was by reason of this conversation that she found the spirit to say 'no'; but she departed from him spiritless. Few as the days were, they had been weighted by many disappointments, and it began to seem to her that she had been in London a long while. Fleet Street, but a week ago an avenue to fame, eloquent of Dr Johnson's suggestion, looked now the least attractive thoroughfare that she had trodden, and Goldsmith's tomb no longer lured her tired footsteps to the Temple. The lives behind the curtains that fronted her attic, across the railings and the brandies of Torrington Square, did not stir her curiosity any more: her own affairs absorbed her when she sat by the window. For all the magnitude of London, the fraction of London that might welcome her was dwindling hourly, was shrinking to the limitations of the village to which she was recommended to return. Her thoughts were concentrated more and more upon *The Aspect*, but she thought of it with diminished confidence; by the light of bland but bootless interviews, the promise of bland letters looked smaller to her. She was far more nervous than sanguine when she presented herself at the office again and inquired if her correspondent had returned.

The office of *The Aspect* was not imposing – it shrunk from observation in an alley, and boasted neither a liveried doorkeeper nor darting boys. She addressed herself to a faded young man behind a counter that looked too long for him; and when he had asked her name he lifted a flap in the counter unceremoniously and went into the next room.

'Mr Savile says, will you go in, please,' he said, reappearing. He held the glass door open for her; and an elderly gentleman, whose smile

113

seemed to her to have a touch of curiosity in it, rose and shook hands with her.

'Miss Moore! How do you do? I'm pleased to make your acquaintance.'

'Thank you,' said Theodosia.

'I'm sorry to have missed you when you called before.'

She sat down in an armchair, which, like all armchairs in the scenes of nervous interviews, had been constructed undesirably. Mr Savile smiled again, and revolving from a beautiful desk that, it occurred to her, would be better placed in her father's study, said, 'So you've come to London, Miss Moore! Er – permanently?'

'I've come chiefly to see you,' she said. 'It *was* you who wrote to me, wasn't it?'

He bowed. 'I am honoured. Yes, it was I who wrote to you. I am the proprietor and editor of *The Aspect*. I was very much interested by your stories, Miss Moore; I found them quite out of the common – very individual. And have you brought something else to show me?'

'No,' she acknowledged regretfully, 'I haven't – I'm not thinking of fiction just now… Mr Savile, I want to find a post – I don't mind what it is — but I want regular work. I've been on a paper already, you know, the –'

'I remember,' he nodded; 'your first manuscript came from the office. As a detail, it was the stationery you wrote on that drew my attention to the manuscript. As a rule, the stories sent in by strangers are read by the assistant editor, but seeing that you weren't a novice, I put yours in my pocket.'

'I thought perhaps the stationery might do some good,' she laughed; 'that was why I wrote to you on it.'

'I gave you credit for the idea at the time. Your connection with the Press is – er – temporarily severed?'

'Yes,' she said pleasantly; 'I've just been discharged for incompetence.'

'Oh! I am grieved to hear that.' He was refreshed – he regarded her with genuine amusement. 'And so you thought you might suit *The Aspect*?'

'And so I hoped The Aspect might come to my rescue. Mr Savile, I've *got* to find something else to do! I thought of you directly; I came here as soon as I arrived, and when they told me you were out of town, I – it wasn't a nice moment at all. The street looked ever so much uglier when I went out than when I came in. Since then I've been trying all the editors that had ever heard of me – I've even tried one or two that hadn't – but I can't find a vacancy anywhere. If *you* won't consider me either, my journey's a failure.'

'But I shall be most happy to consider anything you send me, Miss Moore, I assure you. At any time that you care to let me see a story, it shall receive every attention.'

'Yes,' she said feebly. 'It's very kind of you to say so… but, of course, that leaves me in the same position that I was in before you were good enough to see me. What I want to do is to work as steadily here as I did there – I want a salary.'

The gentleman's attentive attitude was less encouraging. Shorn of friendly phrases and bared to a plain unvarnished tale, his discourse upon the difficulty of her enterprise was a well- intentioned warning that she was unlikely to accomplish it in a month of Sundays. 'What was the nature of the work there?' he asked – 'what feature of the paper did you undertake?'

She mentioned several features that she had undertaken, mentioning them with no enthusiasm, since the face of *The Aspect* was modelled on a different plan. 'But sometimes I did the dramatic criticism,' she added, indicating his opportunity.

'Mr Pritchard is to do our first-night notices in future,' he said, and crushed her with a Name. 'So you sat in judgment, too, did you?'

'That was how I came to grief.'

'Oh?' His eyes twinkled. 'I hope you weren't too severe?'

'Well, I wrote what I thought too candidly, and the chief didn't agree with my opinion. He had no complaint to make of me in any other respect, so far as I am aware, but they found me shockingly incompetent as a dramatic critic.'

'Ah!' He recognised that she was laudably discreet as a discharged journalist. 'What was the play that you objected to, Miss Moore?'

'There had been several differences of opinion,' said Theodosia; 'the crisis was a play called *London Inside Out.*'

'That monument of dramatic art?' He laughed heartily. 'And you ventured to disapprove? Dear, dear! Its fame has even reached *me*.

There's an exemplar for you – if you want to grow rich by authorship, leave literature alone and write masterpieces like *London Inside Out*.'

'Ah!' she murmured. 'But I'm not aspiring to grow rich yet, I'm only ambitious to earn a living.'

In no other office had the conversation been so prolonged as here. Mr Savile's questions led her to speak of her parentage; he referred again very warmly to her work; and by-and-by she was able to gather that the journal was not quite so flourishing a property as she had supposed. It proved to be by no means a dejecting visit, although definitely he said little more than that he would be glad to take a short story from her at the price of a guinea as often as she could offer to him one that he found suitable. There was a tardy allusion to a possible development of the paper – a mere hint that he might perhaps be in a position to discuss a different arrangement a little later on; and, vague as the hint had been, it acquired exciting promise when she inquired presently whether he, like the others, counselled her to beat a retreat and was answered, 'Oh, well, unless you'd find it more convenient to return, I – I think I should remain in town for the next few weeks. Stay in Torrington Square and write some stories! Anything I can publish shall be paid for on acceptance.'

It was the longest and it was the most satisfactory of her experiences. That evening she went to the little post-office round the corner with the first truly hopeful letter that she had sent home since she reached the strange land; and next day when she woke, it was luxurious to remember that she wasn't forced to go out. She projected a tale about a girl like herself in Fleet Street; and, excepting for the luncheon interval, she spent the morning and most of the afternoon in writing some of a tale about a totally dissimilar girl on a farm. She was beginning to lose confidence in the girl and her own abilities, and even in the exciting hint, when a bang at the door preluded an announcement: 'A Mr Tatham was harskin for her.'

She thrust a pin through a hat, and hurried. The pleasure was vivid in the passage, the questions were quick.

'Well?'

'Well?'

She smiled and nodded reassuringly. 'I'm all right. How sunburnt you've got!'

'You haven't been having a bad time? You've been comfortable?'

'No – yes,' she laughed. 'Shall we go into the Square? – there's nowhere to talk in here.'

The key that should have lain on the hatstand wasn't to be seen, but they went across to the gate and stood waiting for someone inside to notice them. The moments were so few before a child ran over the lawn at her signal and let them in, that it was surprising to realise how much he had contrived to ask and to hear on the kerb.

'So it looks hopeful, doesn't it?' she concluded gaily.

'Hurrah!' He wanted to grip her hand again, to slip his arm through hers, as they sauntered along the path. 'I was all wrong; it's a good thing you wouldn't listen to me.'

'Oh, but you said you thought you were wrong – so you were right!'

'Yes, I hedged shamefully, didn't I? I am so glad; I've wondered every day. And the house – have you anybody to talk to?'

'It'll do to go on with. No, there's nobody to say much to; but there wasn't anybody at Mrs Leake's before you came. Oh, it's dull, of course – one can feel much lonelier among the wrong people than all alone – but my room's not bad, and I often come and sit in here. You said the Square would make it nicer for me, didn't you? After Fleet Street on a hot afternoon the key has been a boon and a blessing. At the other end, if you half shut your eyes and take care which way you look, you can almost think it's country. When did you come back? you haven't come from the City so early?'

'I came back this afternoon. No, I don't go hopping again till tomorrow. I thought I'd call at once, in case there was anything I could do – in case anything was wrong.'

Her smile said 'Thank you' prettily. . . .

'Well, you don't tell me if you've enjoyed yourself? Did you leave your mother all right?'

'My mother was a good deal changed,' he said thoughtfully; 'she looks her age now. No, that isn't it! she always looked her age; but she usedn't to talk like it, she usedn't to dress like it – I usedn't to remember how old she was. Now she doesn't pretend any more. She seems to have resigned herself to old age all at once. Of course everybody would say she was quite right, but – but her having done it all at once made it rather pathetic to me to see… No, I didn't enjoy myself particularly – better than *you've* done. It's a pity *The Aspect* man wasn't in town when you arrived, it would have spared you a lot, eh? You've been miserable sometimes?'

She gave a shrug. 'It wasn't so bad where I had had some work taken – that gave me something to say as I went in. The last day or two, when I wasn't sure where to go – I didn't like it then! I asked the way to some paper that didn't look too unlikely, too heavy or distinguished, and when I reached the office – I walked on! There was something about the doorway or the staircase that seemed to say it was no use going in. I looked at shop windows first. Have *you* come across doors like that?'

'All the stage doors up West!' he said. 'Well, you're going to stay, after all?'

'I hope so.'

'So do I! On Saturdays I only hop for half the day; if I might come on Saturday afternoon, I could show you places – I could show you the three places in London where a cup of coffee is to be had; one of them's near Fleet Street, and it's shabby, but cheap. I –' Again he was daunted by the social question. They had sat down, and he scratched hiero-glyphics with his stick on the gravel. 'I wish you knew more about me,' he faltered.

Theodosia said, 'I know you're my friend.'

'I *am*. I'd like to be a very real friend to you if you'll let me. It doesn't sound as if it meant much – a clerk in the City – but if I could do anything for you, I'd do it like a shot.'

'I'm sure you would.'

'I've never had a friend.'

'Before!' said the girl gently.

Tatham looked beyond the railings, seeing no answer to the question. It was instinct, not reason, that urged him to declare his engagement, and his mind groped helplessly for the casual phrase. What tangible difference did it make? Was he to be forbidden friendship because he was engaged to be married? … Instinct reiterated that she must be told. He couldn't see why, but he ceased to rebel against instinct. Turning to her, reluctantly for the first time, he stammered:

118

'You don't think I oughtn't to be friends with you because I'm engaged, do you?'

Suddenly he seemed to her remote – even she too asked of herself what tangible difference it made. The instant impulse of her sex was dissimulation; but deeper, and more significant, was something in her intimating that the moment was painful for him. She realised that the moment was painful for him, and that he was at her mercy, though her brain acknowledged nothing to account for his being at her mercy, nor to explain the strange aspect of the moment.

'You don't think I oughtn't to be friends with you because I'm engaged, do you?'

'Why should I?' She smiled. It appeared to her that she had fulfilled her intention and answered brightly. To him it seemed that a shadow fell between them.

'That's what I thought you'd say.'

'I should like to meet her.'

'I should like you to, very much.' The shadow was darkening; why was he being driven to lie? He added with intense relief, 'She's away now, on tour.'

'Do you mean she's an actress?'

'Yes. We've been engaged for years.'

'That's all the nicer in one way — you must know each other so well.'

'Oh yes.'

'And she can understand your work.'

'Oh yes,' he repeated, labouredly enthusiastic. 'Of course, that's – that's a great thing.'

Not because she saw that he was more to her than she admitted – not because she knew the man and didn't know the girl – simply because she was a woman, it was to the man that her sympathy went out. Maternally she was sorry for his blunder. 'Maternally' is just. But from that point she paltered with perception, averting her eyes from what she didn't wish to see. She didn't wish to see that, since he was to marry a girl who was unsuited to him, companionship might prove in the long run a mistaken kindness. His loneliness cried to her. By no means guiltily, by no means selfishly, she was eager to mitigate the loneliness.

In the road behind them a piano-organ hurled forth an interruption too strident to be ignored, and after her start she welcomed it: 'There's a procession of them all the time; I don't know why the notice-board that says they aren't allowed in the Square isn't taken away – it seems silly to leave it there!'

They moved to another seat, and the tension was past. On both sides there was an argument, ostensibly impregnable – the eternally delusive argument which ignores the fact that man and woman's friendship is the one true and safe foundation for their love.

BOOK III

I

Miss Peggy Harper was to become Mrs Tatham in about three months' time. More than eight months had gone by since Tatham paid his first visit to Torrington Square; and in the meanwhile he had stood by a grave in the Sweetbay cemetery, and the proprietress of a Sweetbay boarding-house had begun to forget her resentment of the 'upset' occasioned by a boarder's dying in the house.

The necessity for proposing that the engagement should materialise, now that his salary would suffice for matrimony on such lines as were familiar to the Harpers, was not the only thing that the interval had displayed to Tatham. Primarily he viewed the fact that he loved another woman, and with all his soul he regretted that he had not summoned the courage to ask Peggy to release him directly the truth was clear. Instead, he had denied himself Miss Moore's companionship in many hours when he had longed for it.

He had denied it to himself now for six weeks on end, and found the applause of conscience inadequate as a substitute. Conscience, indeed, tempered its applause with no little censure at this period. He should have been frank with Peggy! He should have been frank with her last autumn – he should have been frank with her long before that! Conscience, or common sense affirmed that he should have been frank with her before they had been engaged a week. In looking back, it seemed that it would, once, have been a fairly easy thing to do. It seemed that it would have been, comparatively, an easy thing to do at almost any time prior to his mother's death. Afterwards – Only the night after the funeral, he remembered that Mrs Harper had let fall something cheerily and horribly significant! He did not see what he could, in decency, have done after his mother died; from that point, it appeared to him, the marriage had been inevitable.

He made these reflections again as he travelled on the Tube to Islington, the locality of Mrs Harper's latest 'rooms'. It was Sunday, and the girl, once more touring, was due, at some hour today, from Brighton. When Liverpool Road was reached and the door had been opened, a theatrical hamper blocking the passage showed him that she had arrived already, and on the first floor he learnt that she had preceded him by only a few minutes.

'Hallo, Chris,' she cried, 'here I am!' She greeted him in high spirits. Although she hated the bother of letter-writing when she was away, she was always glad to see him on her return – she would have been very dull in London 'without a boy to talk to'. And she was glad that she was going to be married. It was true that, pestered, or taken to task by Naomi Knight last year, she had said that it 'didn't hurt being engaged, and that it was nice to have someone to pay her bus fares when she was in town'; but now, since his mother had 'popped off and he had all his screw to himself' she contemplated the matter from a different point of view. To remember that she would have to go on working for only a few months longer had exhilarated her more highly every time she dwelt upon it; and privately she was of the opinion that a briefer interval between his bereavement and the wedding would have met the case.

'Well, young man, and how are you?' said Betsy Harper. 'When I was engaged to be married and came back from tour, Peggy's pa used to turn up at the station and pay my cab!' There was a touch of acrimony in the banter.

'Now then, mother!'

'Perhaps you wrote him what train you were coming by?' said Tatham drily. 'All I heard was, 'Home on Sunday.''

'Chris is all right,' put in the girl. 'How goes it, Chris? No news, I suppose?'

'Nothing good,' he acknowledged. 'You're looking very fit.'

'Oh, I'm going strong,' she announced, taking off her hat. 'I've had an offer!'

'Yes, I *don't* think!' remarked Mrs Harper.

'Straight!'

'Well, but you don't need any other engagement,' he said; 'this tour doesn't finish for three weeks, does it?'

'Fortnight – Deptford and Hammersmith.'

'What do you mean, she 'doesn't need any other engagement', if she isn't going to get married before August? What's she to live on, do you think? Things aren't so gay with me, I can tell you! Offer for what?'

'The Piccadilly, if you please! How's that?' She turned from the mirror to enjoy the effect. 'A part at the Piccadilly! That'll do to fill in the time, won't it?'

'Go on! you don't so much as know what they're doing at the Piccadilly, you silly kid!'

'I know what the next production's to be – a new comedy of Forsyth's. Give me a cig, Chris, I'm dying for a smoke.' Her nod was emphatic. 'I'm not rotting – it's right enough, He came in to see the show the other night at Brighton; he wrote asking me to go and see him at the Old Ship; he was as sweet as sweet when I went.'

'Forsyth?'

'Talked to me as if he'd been my father!'

Betsy Harper was agape. 'Oh, well, I don't know anything about the business, that's all,' she said; 'I don't know talent when I see it! All right, one lives and learns.' She stared at the girl round-eyed. 'It's the funniest bit *I* ever heard in my life!'

Tatham noted that the maternal disparagement found Peggy less meek than usual on the subject of her abilities. He said quickly:

'Well, she's been paid a pretty substantial compliment. Forsyth is supposed to know as much about the stage as any man alive, isn't he? What sort of part is it, Peggy?'

'Very good,' drawled the girl; and having waited till this intelligence had sunk, she added with a self-conscious smile, 'Lead! ... If you want to know' – she was addressing her speechless mother – 'he told me there wasn't a woman in London that could touch it – he said the stars were all a precious sight too old. He told me I had exactly the right appearance, that I was just the girl he'd been looking for... I'm to go to his house tomorrow, and he's going to read the part to me. The heroine's not supposed to be more than seventeen – she's at school in the first act; he's going to show me just how he wants it played. He's shown me a bit already. He says if I put myself in his hands, he 'guarantees' I can do it – and "make a hit"! There's nothing the matter with Forsyth! you should hear him speak some of his lines — he might have been an actor.'

'He *was* an actor,' faltered Betsy Harper; 'didn't you know that?' The situation was mystifying her less. 'Well, it's a bit of luck and no mistake!

My word, if it had only come along a bit sooner!' There was umbrage in the look she bent on Tatham. 'What do you think of your girl now?' she demanded. '*You* aren't throwing yourself away, my King Cophetua!'

'I never was, Mrs Harper,' he said.

'Ah! some people didn't think so.'

'But, so far as I'm concerned, she can refuse the engagement. She won't go on playing the part after we marry, anyhow.'

'Of course I shan't! Besides, the piece may be off before then.'

'I make you a wager you change your mind, Mister Christopher. Now then, like a bet on it? "Won't go on playing it after you marry"? Yes, I see you advising her to give it up if she's getting big money! You *will* be so flush that your wife's salary won't matter to you, *won't* you? I heard something about you the other day.'

'Oh, something nice?' he murmured.

'No, it wasn't. Something about your plays!' She turned eagerly to her daughter. 'You don't know what terms he's got in his head, Peggy?'

'Well, 'tisn't likely; terms haven't been mentioned yet. They'll be good enough, whatever they are – pay our exes in these digs while I'm here.'

'You leave the contract to *me*,' said Mrs Harper; 'I'm the person to look after that till you're a married woman. Don't you sign anything; *I'll* "talk terms" for you, d'ye hear?'

'Thanks, I can do all that's wanted,' said Peggy sharply. 'I know; you'd go asking too much and queering the job for me.'

'What do you say, miss?'

'I know! 'Tisn't to be expected they'll give me a big chance, and star terms besides. Stands to sense they won't. I don't want it lost by anybody opening her mouth too wide. Now, it's no good, mother!' she exclaimed; and Tatham, who had been apprehensive of an outburst from Mrs Harper, was relieved to see her subside. 'I found this shop for myself, and if I've got to go on working till August, I mean to work where it suits me. I'm not going on tour again – I'm sick of it! I'm going to the Piccadilly.'

'"Found it for herself!"' muttered Mrs Harper. 'Dropped out of the skies into her lap!'

'Very well, then, leave it where it dropped – don't go muffing it.' She glanced towards Tatham for approval. 'What time's tea supposed to come on here? Chris, you may give me another cig, under the circs.'

But the matter was by no means disposed of. The old actress was fully awake now to the fact that a dramatist of importance would find her daughter's childish air a valuable asset for his next play, and the fear that the chance was not to be turned to the best advantage obsessed her. Her emotion was no longer incredulity, nor amazement, nor gratitude – it was greed unadulterated. Thrice she returned, by circuitous routes, to the question of the salary, and Tatham sat nervous of high words occurring after all.

At last, seizing the opportunity afforded by a pause, he put in:

'By the way, who was it who was talking to you about me the other day – what was it he said?'

It served. She regarded him sombrely.

'It was Beaver – if you know who *he* is.'

'The business manager at the Diadem?'

'Oh, you *have* heard as much as that! Yes, I was having a chat with him about you.'

'I suppose he said my comedy wasn't any good?'

'Beaver don't read the pieces – *he* won't look at your comedy, my lord. And no more will anybody else, by all accounts! If you want to know, he told me you were wasting your time sending your manuscripts about the West End – he said he didn't know what you could be think- ing of. "Good gracious!" he said, "the man must be crazy. You don't suppose a high-class management is going to consider anything by the author of *London Inside Out*…" Even if you took another name – even supposing you did get a play done – he said you'd never get a success. The critics'd be sure to hear who you were, and they'd be prejudiced against your work before they went… So that's how much chance *you've* got!'

He neither spoke nor flinched, but his face was colourless. The career of a melodrama which was in the course of time to earn upwards of thirty thousand pounds for its owner, though it had left its author on an office stool, was now notorious in the theatrical world, but this was the first plain intimation he had had that its notoriety was fatal to him.

Often as he had questioned and trembled, it seemed to him, in the sick instant, that the blow took him unawares. 'Wasting his time'! Whatever its qualities, anything he might write was damned in advance. Nothing to hope for — his work wasn't to be read. The clerkship for life!… He went home from the clerkship twenty years hence, and 'home' meant the bitterness of failure, and loneliness, and the remembrance of the right woman…

The shrillness of Peggy's voice jerked him back – the girl was protesting, offering encouragement. The sense of what she was saying began to reach his mind.

'I don't see,' cried Peggy, 'that it matters what you write, if it pays. Let the West End slide, then! Go on writing plays like *London Inside Out*, Chris – that's the best way. If you ask *me*, Beaver's given us a jolly good tip!'

II

He had not known he was going there; his only definite aim, when he got up, was to be alone with his thoughts. As he drew a deep breath outside the house, he was intensely thankful that he had devised an adequate excuse for escaping early. So far from having intended to go to her, he had traversed the dreariness of Pentonville Road afoot, instead of whisking westward by train. It was when he reached King's Cross that desolation clamoured for her. It would not matter what she said; he was not even certain that he wished to speak of what he had heard. As yet he was acutely conscious of nothing but the need of seeing her – he sought only the alleviation of her presence.

She was living in Heathcote Street now. When a tentative appointment on *The Aspect* had begun to acquire the promise of permanency, she had installed herself in furnished apartments. He found her in the tiny parlour with her hat on.

'I'm a nuisance?' he asked. 'You were going out.'

'With nowhere to go!' she said, pulling out the hat-pins promptly. 'The room was getting on my nerves a little, that's all, or perhaps it was the twilight – we'll have the gas; have you a match in your pocket?'

He lit the gas, and she saw and said that he was looking tired.

'Am I?' The mantelshelf was fragrant and vivid with masses of lilac and carnations. There was a bowl of them on the table too. 'You've been very reckless!'

'They came from our garden at home; it's my birthday.'

He wished her 'Many happier returns.'

'It hasn't been festive. I had no idea I should feel so sentimental about it, but I wish it hadn't fallen on Sunday – that made it lonelier…You see, you aren't a nuisance, you're quite a tolerable event.'

She didn't ask him why he had stayed away so long, because she knew.

'It must be a jolly garden,' said the man, picturing her in a garden.

'It isn't very well kept; there are only the girls to look after it, and we leave the daisies on the lawn, but I think it's rather nice. We've a fountain, of sorts; we're very vain of our shabby fountain. It plays the Prince of Wales's feathers – when the water-rate terror hasn't just been;

after we've paid a water rate, we only let it trickle, for a week or two… Oh!' She took up a little stack of typewriting. 'I've read *Shams*. I ought to have sent it back to you. I want to keep it a little longer, though, if I may? I think it's the biggest thing you've done.'

'I'm glad you like it. No, I'm in no hurry to have it back; you can keep it for ever, if you like; you're the only person who'll ever have a good word to say for it!'

The question in her eyes was insistent. He looked away, opened one of the acts and ruffled the leaves, and tossed it back on to the table. 'I've got the blues!' he burst out.

'They're obvious. . . . Bluer than normal, aren't they?' she asked, smiling crookedly.

'I've made a reputation! They say I must be crazy to go on sending my stuff, that nothing with my name on it will ever be looked at in a London theatre from now to the Day of Judgment. I'm labelled a "hack", so nothing I do can ever be worth the paper it's written on – and that's the cheapest sold; nobody's going to turn a page to see what it's like!'

Challenge was in the girl's voice. 'Who's "they"?'

'Oh, a man who ought to know; somebody "inside"; he had no reason to lie about it. He may be wrong, of course, but that's his candid opinion. He told Mrs Harper – who amiably told me. Oh, I don't blame her for telling me, she was quite right to let me know, but I've had a rollicking afternoon.' He tried to laugh. 'So I've dropped in to cheer you up on your birthday – not having been near you for six weeks, while there was nothing worse than usual the matter with me!'

He, too, had kept count of the weeks! Her heart missed a beat.

'Even if he's right –' she began, and perceived that he knew what she was going to say. 'Another name wouldn't help?' she queried.

'So I'm told. He said that, even if I did get something done, the Press wouldn't take it seriously. He said the critics would know whom it was by.'

'How?'

'I don't know. He said it would be bound to leak out. It isn't as if I were just a rotter who'd written failures, you see – I've the distinction of being a rotter who's written muck that everybody has heard of. The idea seems to be that there are crimes so bad that nothing can conceal them – "nor earth, nor sea, though they should be ten thousand fathoms deep"! I don't think the gentleman suggests the critics would have any animus against me, why should they? He means they'd go persuaded that the cloven foot was going to show and that they'd find what they were jolly well looking for. "The dialogue is passable, but the melodramatic nature of the theme –" or "The theme is pleasant, but the author's experience of provincial melodrama –" To –' He choked. 'I wish the damned thing were – I beg your pardon!'

The hands in her lap rose and fell with a little futile gesture. It was the first time that she had seen him despair, and – not because she loved, love may be inept – because she was an artist she understood. Her gaze turned to the thing of brains and typewriting on a garish table-cover, and for comfort she tapped it.

'Some day!' she prophesied. 'You'll see! The name you're afraid of is going to 'mean things' some day. I don't say it because we're friends – I've told you I didn't like some of your things. But some day, in places like this, nobodies like us will be wishing they were Christopher Tatham, and yearning as you yearn now.'

He walked up and down the room, the room that was so limited that five short steps took him from the window to the shiny chiffonier.

'Everything's a fraud!' he exclaimed. '"Yearn"? It's a big word for a trumpery ambition. Yes, of course, I want to get on. I want to make my way, it's a man's duty, but recognition isn't everything. It wouldn't mean happiness. It sounds like sour grapes. But one changes. It's extra-ordinary how one changes! I wanted to be an actor once – it wouldn't give me any pleasure now. It isn't the footlights that dazzle me today. If I could succeed in any capacity at all! – I write because it's the only thing I can do; I'm not satisfied to jog along as a clerk all my life, that's what it amounts to. I want a career. I want a career because I've nothing else to look forward to... *You know*!' He flung round at her as if she had protested. 'You *know* I've made a mess of it! I wasn't in love with her the night I proposed; I didn't mean to propose. It happened. Well, I've stuck it — honour or cowardice, I don't know – I've stuck it, and I suppose I've got to go through with it, she's waited for me so many years; but if I'm to fail in love, and everything else as well – Do you think it's too late? Look here, we're pals, aren't we? I want a pal's advice. I'm fond of somebody else. I don't know whether she cares for me. I mustn't ask her – yet; she wouldn't tell me if I did ask her; but I could be happy, even as a clerk, as long as I lived, if I could go home in the evening to the other woman… That's the situation; that's how I feel! What's the straight thing for me to do?'

He didn't say, 'I love you,' she didn't say, 'I understand.' When she trusted her voice and found that it broke, she whispered:

'It *is* too late.'

'Why?'

'Five years – six years, what is it? She must care for you a good deal to have waited so long as that… And don't forget that the other woman mayn't care in the same way.'

'If she did?' he urged, drawing closer to her.

'It would make no difference – in my opinion.'

'Not if I were free – if I could go to her honestly tomorrow and tell her I was free?'

'If she'd any self-respect, she'd be ashamed of herself: she'd think of the girl that she had made miserable; she'd think of the girl almost as much as she thought of *you*. If she's – if she's worth wanting, she wouldn't find the position good enough!'

'*That's* how it seems to you?' he said.

She nodded. 'That's how it seems to me. I can't answer for *you*; you're a man, you might break it off and feel no regret – I can't say. I don't know Miss Harper, and I can't pretend to shape your future, but I *can* put myself in the place of the other woman – it wouldn't take you any nearer to *her*!'

After a long silence, he said harshly :

'I suppose I may as well stick it altogether, then. It's hardly worth-while to behave like a cad for nothing… I've been a cheerful visitor! Do you know, I think I'll say "good night".'

Both knew that it meant 'goodbye.'

'Good night,' she said, white-faced and smiling.

The few seconds seemed insufferably long before the slam of the street door and the sound of retreating footsteps made it safe for her to give way.

III

The precise number of more talented and ambitious young women who would have welcomed ecstatically the chance that had befallen a young woman possessing only mediocre ability, and no ambition at all, cannot be stated. But some scores of them were, at the time, seeking the humblest of engagements vainly. And when it is said that W.B. Forsyth had gone to Brighton expressly to see Peggy Harper, and rejoiced in his fauteuil, the situation may appear more anomalous still.

Forsyth's thanksgiving, however, was not inspired by admiration of Miss Harper's histrionic capabilities. He was under no impression that he had discovered a genius, nor, as a dramatist of experience and reputation, was he in the habit of exploring for geniuses – he found it a far more profitable policy to cast established favourites in his plays. He had gone to Brighton because he had been suffering, for the past three months, from a sensation not widely removed from panic, a liability to wake in the night and ask himself, with an all-gone feeling in the stomach, why he had been so rash as to devote a year to the writing of a piece which demanded for its adequate interpretation a personality possessed by no actress that he could call to mind. In fine, for the first time since he had attained a position, Forsyth had done an unpractical thing; his theme – most promising in the scenario – had lured him to in- discretion. The chief, the big part was, of course, a man's, since the play had been designed for the Piccadilly Theatre, and Onslow, the actor-manager, was to be the hero; but the hero had a daughter, 'Daphne', and, as the work developed, 'Daphne' had taken unto herself an importance for which her progenitor had been unprepared at the outset. To reduce the daughter would be to detract from the father – to detract from the father would be to spoil the play.

Forsyth, the eminent, had appealed to a dramatic agent with an anxiety as keen as the agent's poorest client. The harassed playwright had viewed photographs by the dozen, and made fatiguing journeys to view some of the originals. He had been to Kingston-on-Thames to see a girl who was actually as young as 'Daphne' was supposed to be, but she had comported herself with all the stiff timidity of the stage novice, and he had realised, even while he deplored, that she wasn't to be trained in the few weeks at his disposal. 'You'll never find every quality you want!' Mrs Forsyth had reminded him, when he returned despondent to announce that the journey had been waste of time; and he had answered, 'I don't suppose I shall, my dear, but I can't have an ungainly Daphne; I'd rather have any defect than ungainliness!' He had travelled to Cheltenham to see another girl, who would have recommended herself to him but for the fact that she weighed too much; and again his wife had mentioned the unlikelihood of his securing the ideal exponent of the part. 'I can't have an adipose Daphne,' he had said; 'I'm willing to put up with anything but adiposity!' Miss Harper was not too stout, nor too tall, nor too short; her voice had some pleasant notes in it, and would be very agreeable when he had taught her how to use it; and, during the interview at the hotel, she had impressed him as being plastic material. He was infinitely relieved; and so was Mrs Forsyth, who had found him latterly 'gey ill to live with'.

When Peggy made her toilette on the afternoon after her return to town, her mother wandered about the room querulously.

'You'll be sorry when it's no good if you don't leave it to me,' she said; 'you'll go too cheap, mark my words! You've no idea what you ought to get – how *should* you have? You've never seen a salary worth talking about. I suppose if they offered you five pounds a week you'd take it?'

'You bet I should!' said the girl.

'What?'

'I'd a jolly sight rather have five pounds a week in London than thirty bob on tour! What do *you* think?'

She continued to array herself complacently. All her belongings were not unpacked yet, and alternately she searched for trifles in the chest of drawers, and dived for finery in the hamper.

'Some people don't deserve to have any luck – some people don't know luck when they see it! My word, you with a mother that knows the ropes, talking about five pounds a week! You little fool, you!'

'Mind, please, mother, you're getting in the way!'

'Oh, I'll mind — mind my own business, too! What does it matter to *me* if you throw your chance away?' Her arms were dramatic. 'What does it matter to me, now you're going to get married? That's it, that's the way – pinch and strain for your girl all your life, and then as soon as a bit of luck comes to her, off she goes to a fellow!'

Peggy contemplated two pairs of soiled kid gloves. 'I don't know whether to put on the white or the fawn,' she said. 'Which do you think would go best? Chris says white gloves are "noisy".'

'Chris be bothered,' snapped Mrs Harper. 'Put on the white! What does Chris know? I'm fed up with your Chris. A nice soft thing for *him*, won't it be, to have a wife to keep him?'

'He won't have a wife to keep him, because he wants me to leave the profession, and you know it very well – so don't talk rot, mother! I don't know why you've got your knife into him all of a sudden,' she went on sharply. 'You liked him very much once; he hasn't changed, so far as I can see!'

'No, and never will – he's a sticker, that's what he is. Never do any good as long as he lives.'

'That's as may be,' said the girl defiantly. 'Look here, stop it ! I don't want a row, I've got something else to think about today. Stop it,' she repeated, with a catch in her voice, 'coming and nagging me just when I want to go out looking my best!'

She surveyed herself in the mirror again, and slipped some more shilling bangles on her wrists. A vulgar hat aggravated a vivid blouse, made at home and made badly. Her reflection encouraged her, and the occasion was sufficiently exciting for her to recover her spirits almost as soon as she was in the street. By the light of an offer for a fashionable theatre, the detested profession looked already less odious to her, and she was at one with her mother in deeming it a thousand pities that such advancement had not occurred to her a long time ago. The tears and troubles that she would have been spared! Why couldn't somebody have seen a few years earlier how clever she was?

Wouldn't Naomi Knight, and Nelson, and everybody else that she had ever met be astonished when they saw the news in *The Stage*! She smiled broadly on the pavements of Liverpool Road in imagining their ejaculations. 'Lor, look at this, Peggy Harper goes to the Piccadilly!' In the bus another girl, obviously an actress, sat, adorned with cheap finery and jingling with bangles; it was exhilarating to surmise that she was going up West to try to find an engagement in a No. 2 company.

'She wouldn't half like to have an appointment with Forsyth, would she?' mused Peggy. 'What ho!'

But a tessellated entrance and the splendour of the hall-porter were a shade intimidating. Though she had visited many a person whose abode was called a 'flat', Forsyth's was the first flat that she had seen.

Her embarrassment was dispelled by the great man's greeting; his pleasure was evident as he welcomed her. No repugnant detail of her costume escaped his notice, but her taste in dress mattered nothing to him, for 'Daphne's' frocks would come from Bond Street, and Mrs Forsyth would take 'Daphne' to order them; he again appraised the eyes, the smile, and the alert little form. If only the imitative faculty lay behind that pretty brow she would serve his purpose well!

At his request she laid the hat aside. He put a typewritten part in her hands, and lolled on a couch, with an act of the comedy on his knees.

'Now we'll take the first scene between Daphne and her father,' he said. 'I told you in Brighton, didn't I, how she feels towards her father? The child's tremendously fond of him, and there's a touch of the protective instinct in her love. You know – that inborn maternal instinct that little girls have for their dolls! Well, Daphne is to show a touch of the maternal when she first suspects that her father is in trouble.'

Peggy nodded, not feeling at all sure, however, what little girls and their dolls had to do with it.

She and Forsyth read the scene aloud, and the dramatist did not once interrupt her. This seemed flattering, and at the end she looked round for a compliment. His face was placid, but she could discern no approval in it. Her heart sank, and as a matter of fact she had read the part much less intelligently than he had expected. He was telling himself that he had hoped for too much at the first attempt, though actually he had hoped for very little. Well, never mind! he was going to mould her into the character, train her in every inflexion, every movement, every flash of facial play. Being tactful and understanding human nature, especially human nature as it was to be found in the wings, he did not at this point say anything to detract from the girl's self-esteem; he allowed the events of the afternoon to do it by degrees.

For three hours he laboured with Peggy, laboured incessantly, disguising the obstinacy of a man who knows what he wants, and means to have it, under a demeanour of unruffled patience.

But the interruptions were countless now, and she was inclined to resent them.

'You promised to put yourself in my hands,' he reminded her once gently.

'Yes – I know, I *am*!' she declared, reddening. 'But – but aren't I to show *any* individuality, then?'

For an instant the professional jargon of the pupil tempted the master to an ironic reply. But he only said, 'Well! perhaps my own idea might be bettered – show me what you want to do there, speak the lines your own way!'

Peggy hadn't a notion of what she wanted to do; she only knew that she was finding this little man with a big head very exacting and wearisome. So she re-read the lines and emphasised words at random, and introduced a laugh, which was musical, but preposterous in a pathetic passage.

'You laugh very prettily,' said Forsyth; 'but, you know, you're supposed to be on the verge of tears there. And I don't care for your emphasis, "I wonder if he sees how *unhappy* I am sometimes." You've already said you're unhappy. It should be "I wonder if he *sees* how unhappy I am sometimes."'

Peggy spoke the words again, but missed the note of pathos.

'Too cheerful,' said Forsyth. 'Remember what she's thinking about. And – Well, never mind that now!' His brain buzzed.

Peggy sighed and persevered.

'Not quite,' he murmured, and delivered the lines several times, very slowly, for her benefit… 'Not quite,' he said again and again; 'now once more! Listen to me and say it just as I do… No, that's a little too whiny!… No, now we're getting a little too coy!… Oh, we shall manage it, don't be afraid! Take your time, there's nothing to be discouraged about. "I wonder if he *sees* how unhappy I am sometimes."'

She echoed him at last; but later, when they returned to the page, the inflexion had been lost, and the lesson had to be given to her again.

And then she kept saying 'inter*est*ing'.

There were many such stumbling-blocks; so many that if any layman had been present he would have marvelled that the playwright could retain confidence in his choice. And more than once Forsyth did waver. He wavered, but he increased his efforts as he questioned forlornly where a likelier 'Daphne' was to be found. And, after all, the girl had grit! When she had recovered from the first shock of disillusion, he could see that she was plucky. While he feigned to be unaware that she was feeling humiliated, he was conscious that a smarting vanity made her task more difficult.

They read no further than the first scene, but they read it so often that at last she knew some of the lines by heart. This led him to play the scene with her, and now, more than ever, she appreciated the qualities of her coach. Not only could he show her how lines should be uttered, he could show her what to do while she said them – and how to convey a tense moment without saying anything at all. He could do more than explain, he could demonstrate.

'No, not like that,' he would say; 'like this!' A little man with a big head simulating a young girl – and simulating so cleverly that he was illustrative and not ridiculous! She was being instructed by a dramatist who, as he wrote, heard every tone and saw every gesture of his characters; she was being drilled in her calling by a dramatist who had been an actor and could indicate in action what he meant. He made no more appeals to intelligence, he talked no longer of the instinct of the girl-child for the doll; he recognised that *she* was the doll, and that it was his business to make her dance. Every finger that she was to lift he showed her; every step that she was to stir. Sometimes he would cry to her not to stir at all. 'It isn't wanted,' he would say, the big head to one side like a photographer's; or, 'No, no, your face can do all that's necessary there. Like this!… *My* face isn't pretty, but I want *yours* to do that.' And presently it would be, 'Now smile, with your hands behind you – tip your chin a little bit. There you are! No; I want the smile more arch… The chin a *leetle* more up… That's it. Now do that again, while you're speaking the line… Capital! very fetching and natural.' The third time that he pulled the wires she began to think complacently that it was natural to her.

The sunshine had faded while they worked.

'We've done enough for today.' He pushed her gently into a capacious chair. 'You've been a very good girl.' Her type was familiar to him, and he gave her the sugar that she craved. 'A very clever girl! Now lean back and curl up. Don't think any more; we're going to have tea.'

The quietest servant that she had ever seen appeared with tea, and tea was served as smartly as if the study had been a 'set' at a West End theatre.

'Cream?' asked the eminent host; and she nearly said, 'Rather!'

She began to examine things, things that she had been too nervous, or too busy, to examine before. Forsyth did himself well, she reflected. What a lovely chair! And that – what-was-its-name? – all over mother-of-pearl and gimcracks! Funny not to have a looking-glass on the mantelpiece, though. Rather dull, the room, but good; oh yes, everything in it was decidedly good. Except, perhaps, the pictures: the pictures didn't seem to have been finished. Her gaze reverted to the celebrity. His attention was concentrated upon a basket of petits-fours, and petulantly he exclaimed, 'Whenever we have these little ding-dongs for tea, there's every sort but the one I like!' Just as Chris might have grumbled, she thought. It thrilled her with a sense of importance to realise that she had heard W.B. Forsyth grumble about his cakes.

He arranged with her that she should come again on the morrow, and every day, and he sent her back to Islington in a taxi-cab, saying that she looked tired. She looked, in truth, a great deal less tired than he – and with reason.

'Well' – Betsy Harper had grown more genial – 'how did the reading go? Was he satisfied with you?'

'Sent me home in a taxi!' boasted Peggy, suppressing much that was unessential to the narrative.

IV

During the weeks that lay between his preliminary lesson to her and the date on which the general rehearsals of the piece began, she had been taught more of the technique of her calling than she had acquired unaided in ten preceding years. She had not been metamorphosed into a clever actress – it was as far beyond his power to instil a gift for histrionics as to communicate a talent for dramatic authorship – but what he had done, with experience and fortitude and the sweat of his brow, was to compel her to mimic him as 'Daphne' with sufficient fidelity for him to foresee her giving a pleasing performance by the time the general rehearsals finished.

It had been a lofty moment when she tripped past the doorkeeper of a West End theatre with a part in her hand for the first time; but, on the whole, the rehearsals at the Piccadilly proved much less gratifying than she had expected. During a quarter of an hour of friendless waiting, while she recognised the popular Miss Marshall, and saw her greet Carrie Warne, and watched Miss Warne chatting intimately with Miss Eley Sashbourne – while she stood envying their clothes, and their air of being at ease here – she had assumed that she would be admitted to the distinguished groups as soon as the prominence of the part that she was to play had been revealed to them. But she was not admitted and made to feel at home. The flash of pride at finding herself on a stage with women who bore names that had been familiar to her all her life, names that were of immense importance to her mind, had expired when she realised that the prominence of her part was resented. Miss Marshall and Miss Warne, who had grown middle-aged without attaining to 'leading business' in London, owed their hard-won reputations to their abilities; and even Miss Eley Sashbourne, who had had rich parents to entertain useful people and buy a position for her, had been satisfied to make her West End debut in a part comparatively small. No cordial welcome was extended to an unknown girl thrust into the position of leading lady. Some of the men offered cheery comments from time to time, but the women remained formal. When she blundered in a scene, the cold condescension of the 'Pardon me, I think you should be on my *left*, my dear!' intimated unmistakably that she should be in the provinces; and when it happened that Forsyth or Onslow corrected her with a touch of temper, she knew that her discomfiture was being regarded in the wings with satirical smiles.

And as the date fixed for the production drew near, both the author and the actor-manager's severity increased. So far from being uplifted now, she thought with tender regret of the happy-go-lucky companies that she had left. Never had she imagined that so much fuss could be made about trifles; and if it had not been too late she would have refused to fulfil the engagement and hidden herself from her mother's wrath. She hated everybody – hated the women for holding aloof from her, hated Forsyth for burdening her, with the responsibility, hated Onslow for 'getting her so cheap'! She entered the theatre pale with apprehension; and since no maternal sympathy was to be looked for, she made a confidant of Tatham, and found him, at this period, newly and strangely companionable.

There was one occasion on which she broke down. The rehearsal had been called for eight o'clock in the evening, and all had gone smoothly until she spoke a line which, by reason of the daily reproofs that it entailed, had become a haunting terror to her. It occurred in a scene with Onslow in the fourth act, and her heart thumped as she approached it. She had repeated it to herself fifty times during the afternoon and felt confident that at last the desired inflexions had been mastered; but now misgivings made her feel sick again.

Onslow, wearing an expression of fatherly solicitude, sat by a table, his forehead resting on a forefinger. She took the three timid steps behind him that she had been drilled to take, and as her voice smote the silence, it seemed to her anxiety that the theatre held its breath to listen. She said:

'I don't know how to tell you what I want to say – I never thought that I should want to say it.'

Onslow's back was declamatory – she knew that she had failed again before he raised a despairing arm towards the roof. The gesture relieved him, his verbal remonstrance was not violent. He inquired with depth of feeling, and of nobody in particular, 'Isn't it marvellous?'

Of her he inquired, 'Are we *never* going to have it right?'

He rose, and dominated the stage – she had no longer a 'father', she had only an actor-manager struggling to control his fury.

'Will you speak it like this, Miss Harper, please? "I don't know how to tell you."'

'"I don't know how to tell you,"' she said, swallowing convulsively.

'No!' His chest heaved under the restraint that he was putting upon expletives, 'Not, "How to tell you" but "How to tell you."'

'"How to tell you,"' she quavered.

He plunged his hands in his trousers pockets and took a little composing turn in front of the footlights.

'Try again, my child! Now, now, now, don't upset yourself; just echo me, that's all I want you to do.' The suavity of his 'all'! 'Listen! "How to tell you."'

Desperation stumbled within a semi-tone of it.

'That's better,' he said encouragingly. 'Now take it a little further: "I don't know how to tell you what I want to say."'

'"I don't know how to tell you what I want to say,"' she wailed. A tear was trickling down her nose.

'It's the most extraordinary thing I ever came across in my life!' gasped Onslow to Forsyth, who was suffering in the stalls. 'We've had three weeks of it!' And in the wings Miss Marshall remarked under her breath to Miss Warne, 'If he engages girls as leading ladies simply because they're *young* –' And, under her breath, Miss Warne answered Miss Marshall, 'When *I* went into the profession, she'd have been playing the servant!' Peggy did not dare to turn her head and didn't catch their words, but she could hear their whispers, and imagined their eyebrows and their shoulders. With all her sobbing soul she yearned to be back on tour in *No Child to Call Her 'Mother'*.

It was nearly one o'clock in the morning before the ordeal reached its climax.

'Bring me a chair!' called Onslow, declining to perceive that a chair was within arm's length of him. 'I'll have it spoken the way I want it, if we all stop in the theatre till breakfast-time!' Then leisurely he sat down and folded his arms; and while the company stood around disconsolate and thought of their cab fares to the suburbs, the actor-manager continued to reiterate, 'I don't know how to tell you what I want to say –

140

I never thought that I should want to say it,' and, blind with tears, Peggy continued to recite the line after him, without catching the right inflexions once.

Finally he leapt out of the chair with more volatility than he had manifested since the days when he played in farce.

'Eleven o'clock tomorrow!' he flung at the prompter.

And, 'I wish I was dead and buried!' she snivelled to Tatham, who was waiting outside to take her home.

He was as sorry for her as if she had been his child – she seemed to him a little futile child, as she panted and sniffed beside him on the deserted pavements till a hansom crawled into view. He reminded her that her misery wouldn't last – that even if she never spoke the line in the way desired of her, the heavens wouldn't fall; he dwelt, as optimistically as his thoughts permitted, on the fact that 'Daphne' was the last part she was to play and that soon she would be his wife. She came nearer to loving him than she had ever done before, as he tried to console her during the long drive. But her sobs persisted, and while she clung to him, she repeated again and again, 'I wish I was dead and buried, I do! I give you my word, I wish I was dead and buried!'

V

Although Forsyth was one of the most accomplished of living dramatists, and an intellectual man, and his play represented some years of
thought and twelve months of strenuous work, it scored only a semi-
success. The Press objected to it on the grounds of 'false psychology',
and the public, who were not in the least concerned with the truth of its
psychology, objected to it because they found it dull. His play fell flat.
But his marionette was exalted. The notices were an ovation to 'Miss
Peggy Harper'. Her 'acute sensibility and intelligence', the 'spontaneity
of her talent', and the 'brilliant promise of her surprising youth' were
commonplaces in panegyrics which sparkled with such phrases as
'sweetly delicious with the winsomeness of English maidenhood' and
a 'career to be conspicuous in the annals of the Stage'.

'Gawd!' gasped Peggy, reading one of the most laudatory of the
criticisms in bed the day after the piece was produced, and wondering
what a lot of the words meant. She could not determine whether she
was being extolled for her 'artistry' in having done something not
clearly expressed, or for her 'artistry' in avoiding it; but no matter which
way it might be, it was evident that she was a unique young creature,
and she felt breathless and a little light-headed. She did not know
whether she wanted to sing, or dance, or cry, but she knew that she
didn't want her bacon, and that the world had altered. There was an
unfamiliar and emotional brightness in the sunshine that streamed into
the untidy room, and never before had she seen her mother sitting at
the edge of the bed, beaming down at her like this. She kicked her heels
hysterically on the mattress.

'Here, I say! run out and buy some more papers, mother,' she
commanded. 'This isn't half all right, what? What price the other
women, now, them and their side? They must be feeling a bit silly this
morning, ain't they? Look here – two lines at the beginning I've got,
and… six, seven, eight, further down. All about *me*!… And Eley
Sashbourne's only got two!' She counted again, and shrieked with
triumph. 'Seven words for the "great" Marshall, and *they* don't weigh
much… Now let's see Warne's little bit… Go on, get some more
papers, mother, blow the expense!'

Tatham's message of pleasure and congratulation delighted her; she felt very tender towards him as she slipped it under the pillow. He had been among the audience, in an undesirable seat, and congratulated her at supper, but until he opened his newspaper at breakfast he had had no idea that he had witnessed a success so noteworthy and brilliant. He telegraphed lengthily to her on his way to the City; and being unable to reach her before she left for the theatre, he waited for her again at the stage-door after the curtain fell.

She joined him radiant and gabbling. Both had read many criticisms in the meanwhile. She kept inquiring if he had seen what this, that, and the other paper said of her. She had scarcely a suspicion that praise in one quarter was more important than in another; she did not know the names of any of the critics, and estimated the value of approval by its superlatives. A daily for which Pritchard wrote the first-night notices, had contained little more about her than 'A very pleasing performance was given by a newcomer to London, Miss Peggy Harper,' and she said contemptuously that she 'didn't think much of that'. She 'didn't think much' of two or three temperate opinions that would have raised her to a pinnacle of rapture a day or two before. Vanity may attain no larger dimensions in the atmosphere of the footlights than elsewhere, but nowhere else does it grow so plentifully, or so fast. The contrast between her celebrity this evening – for 'celebrity' she already had – and her whimpering despair a few evenings ago flared to the man as they walked towards a cab.

'Who'd have thought it?' he exclaimed – 'do you remember our coming along here the other night?'

He was surprised to see, by her shrug, that the reminder was unwelcome. 'Oh, that didn't amount to much!' she said shortly. And something in his tone had displeased her – as the glimmer of amusement in Onslow's eyes had displeased her when he felicitated her on her 'laurels'; and as an undercurrent of facetiousness in her mother's jollity had displeased her all the afternoon.

On the morrow, Forsyth's 'Well, my child, you didn't put up with it all for nothing, eh?' displeased her in the same way. She reflected that it was 'a funny thing' by which she meant 'an annoying one' that 'people' seemed to give her very little credit for the success that she had made;

she was told how lucky she had been, and how grateful she ought to be, but nobody that she met said how clever she was! At the show, of course, the women were hating her for cutting them out; and poor old Forsyth must be feeling a bit jealous – the critics had thought a heap more of her than of him! But even in Chris's congratulations there had been something wrong, something – well, there had been something missing, a touch of the – Of course one could never say such a thing, but really and truly, a touch of the *respect* that her triumph demanded! Naturally, she didn't want him to feel small when he talked to her, but it was funny that he could remain so free-and-easy, all the same!...

It crossed her mind that perhaps he felt more deference than he was disposed to let her see. She reflected that he was 'ever so much' older than she, and a failure – and look what Beaver had said about his things!... Yes, poor old Chris must be feeling a bit out of it, too. Rather sickening for poor old mother, as well, come to think of it! Oh, well, she'd never let on that she was aware of having walked over both their heads, she wasn't that sort. *She'd* never swank, like some people. Nobody could call it 'swank' the way she was behaving to Warne, and Marshall, and Eley Sashbourne now that they 'couldn't help being civil to her; getting a bit of her own back, that was all! Still it was pretty rotten of poor old Chris and poor old mother to pretend they didn't *know* she had risen far above them; they didn't do themselves any good by that!

It was rather less than a week after her debut at the Piccadilly, that when Forsyth stopped to speak to her in the Haymarket she replied to him in the stuffy tone of the highly consequential, and took leave of him with a nod familiar and abrupt. About the same time, her dresser remarked to the young woman behind the pit bar that the 'notices in the pipers had given Miss 'Arper such a swelled head that she couldn't get it through her skirt'.

She was 'eighteen' still. London was informed that she was 'only eighteen' every time that a photograph of her was reproduced in a picture journal – and her photographs were nearly as popular with the picture journals as if she had been a musical-comedy idol. More than half of the audience were drawn to the Piccadilly by their curiosity to witness the performance of 'the winsome English maiden' whose natural talent had swept her to theatrical fame direct from the 'classroom of a fashionable boarding-school' – variously stated to have been in Hanover, Paris, and Eastbourne. A paragraph, under 'Prominent Persons', described Onslow's discovery of her – 'As the favourite of the school finished her recitation, the famous actor-manager turned to his companion, saying, "That child is destined to be one of the greatest actresses of our time."' And the Editor of *Mother And Girls* begged for the privilege of including her views among 'other notable Englishwomen's' upon the Female Suffrage movement. Not being quite sure what it was, and appreciating the value of an additional advertisement, she was harassed, until her mother came to her aid. 'Miss Peggy Harper, the gifted young actress at the Piccadilly Theatre', wrote: 'My time is far too much occupied by my work for me to trouble my head about such matters.' And readers could divine the gifted young actress's weary smile as she thought of the women whose less momentous pursuits allowed them leisure for such frivolities.

The little mummer who had once averred that 'acting was silly' and pronounced her profession 'a rotten business' soon afterwards began to refer to her 'work' and her 'art' in conversation too. Her conversation was decorated with all the phrases which had been impressive to her upon the lips of others – phrases by which she, in her own turn, sought to be impressive at home.

Invariably now she referred to Forsyth as 'W.B.' and she spoke of several distinguished persons to whom she had been presented for a moment behind the scenes, or whom she had never met at all, by their Christian names. To Tatham the affectations that broke out over her nature like a rash were occasionally so exasperating that he marvelled at her mother's blandness. But Betsy Harper, for so long as she could keep sober, or became intoxicated amiably, was minded to avoid dissension with a profitable daughter.

A simple incident which afforded the girl considerable pleasure occurred on a Wednesday. There being no Wednesday matinée at the Piccadilly, she was always free on that day to attend a matinée elsewhere, and highly agreeable it was to her to saunter into the stalls when the house was filled and note that there were ardent playgoers present who recognised her. She unfailingly turned an abstracted gaze towards the pit before she sat down. One Wednesday, as she and her mother entered the foyer of the Sceptre, her glance alighted on young Nelson, waiting among a little group of obscure professionals till he had an opportunity for asking at the box-office if the acting manager could 'oblige him with a seat'. The boy observed her with a start, and sweeping off his hat, regarded her diffidently. When she paused, it was plain that he was delighted to be seen greeting the new star in the foyer of a London theatre.

'Why, Miss Harper!' he exclaimed, for those close at hand to hear, 'how d'ye *do*?'

She was gratified both by his exaggerated bow and his respectful 'Miss Harper' – it proclaimed instantly his appreciation of the fact that they were now in disparate spheres. She tendered limp finger-tips – the fingers that had stroked his face when he called her 'Peggums'.

'Ah, Nelson!' she said, with gracious languor; 'going in to see the show?'

'If I can get a seat,' murmured young Nelson, shooting his linen, and posing with his cane. 'I suppose you've got yours?'

'Oh yes,' she said stuffily, 'I 'phoned that I'd be in.' She had written a request for tickets in the ordinary way, and enclosed a stamped and addressed envelope for the reply, but she had heard Onslow say, in speaking of some other performance, 'I 'phoned that I'd be in,' and had liked the lordly sound of it.

'You're no end of a swell, eh?' He eyed her admiringly. 'My best congrats! I was in front last week.'

'Ah, it's not really very much of a part – one does what one can with it!' She owed this flower of speech to Miss Eley Sashbourne.

'*I* thought it was a ripping part,' said young Nelson. 'I saw your photo in the *Sketch* last week – a whole page to yourself, what! A jolly fine photo it is!'

'It?' she said vaguely. 'Which? I forget... *Sketch*? I don't remember which one they had. There have been so many of me; they're all over London.' She simpered, with a pucker on her brow. 'It's getting rather dull for me to look at the papers now. I can't pick one up without seeing myself – I'm getting so bored by me!'... She acquired a weary, confidential note, her eyebrows climbing higher still. 'You know, it's funny

146

how soon one gets used to it all. I mean to say, one always supposed that fame must be so awfully jolly, but, 'pon my word, there's nothing in it – rather a nuisance in some ways. Wherever I go, I'm stared at. . . Nelly was saying the same thing only the other night.'

Young Nelson smiled uncomfortably. She was talking down to him from such an eminence that he was tempted to improvise an ear-trumpet, and beg her to shout. Later, at the Crown, Peckham, he asserted that he had done so and 'scored off her like billy oh!' Actually, he only faltered 'Nelly'? with interrogation; whereat she said, 'Yes, Ellen Terry. Well, I must skip! Glad to seen you,' and forgot to shake hands.

She wished, ridiculously, that 'fame', in truth, were tedious to her; she had wished it often – of her silly wish had been born her unconvincing lie. The ruffled rose-leaf in her sensational bouquet was the zest with which she inhaled it, for it reminded her how unused she was to popularity. It seemed to her that the one thing needful to set the seal upon her success was, that it shouldn't enrapture her so much; it seemed to her that it must be grand and glorious to be so habituated to adulation that it had lost its thrill, that it left one listless, cold, and sated. She longed to be blasé.

She invited the pit patrons to a view of her, full face, as usual, before settling herself in her seat; and even while she yielded to the temptation, was regretful – not of the fatuity of her conceit, but of the gusto of her youth.

VI

Another of the phrases that commended themselves to her taste was, 'That sort of thing' as a label for the class of dramatic entertainment with which she had hitherto been associated.

'That sort of thing' was eloquent of immeasurable space between the speaker and the disparaged depths. She was aware, with discomfiture, that her future husband was, conspicuously, a creator of 'That sort of thing'. When, by a passing reference, his melodrama was scoffed at in the dressing-room one night – '*London Inside Out*, and that sort of thing!' – she did not say, 'I'm engaged to Mr Tatham.' She went on pencilling her scanty eyebrows and simulated unconcern.

Of course, she meant to marry 'poor old Chris' – that she should ever marry anybody else after all these years, was unthinkable – but, 'For mother's sake', she suggested to him that the wedding should be postponed until Christmas. She explained, with a kiss, that 'for her to clear out and get married the moment her luck had turned would be awfully rough on poor old mother.' And, for another thing, the run of Forsyth's piece was coming to an untimely end, and it was more than likely that in August she would be up to her eyes in the rehearsals of a new part. 'It would be a fearful muddle to get married at the same time.'

There was no longer any allusion between her and Tatham to her leaving the stage. She was now in a position to demand a large salary, and considering the dimensions of his own, he could not dwell on his wish that she should sacrifice the prospect. Already it was manifest to him that her mother's prediction was to be fulfilled – he would be the 'husband of Miss Peggy Harper'. His assent to the proposal that he should possess his soul in patience until Christmas, was forthcoming with such readiness that, if the girl's new egotism had been less prodigious, she would have been wounded in the perception that she was undesired.

They had discussed the matter at the window in Liverpool Road. Beneath them, Islingtonians passed stiffly in their Sunday black, and in the bedroom Mrs Harper was taking a siesta. Peggy's spirits had risen; she was feeling much tenderer towards 'poor old Chris' now that she was not to marry him so soon. She forsook her chair for his knee, and thought what a 'good fellow' he was, and that it was an 'awful pity that he wasn't cleverer'. As often as she laid her artificialities aside and was once more the outspoken little gamine that he had known, it was easier for him to fondle her. A tepid affection, stimulated by gratitude for the unexpected respite that she had afforded him, was animating conversation gaily, when she exclaimed, with a sudden change of tone:

'Oh, bother! I forgot! Naomi Knight's coming in this afternoon. I do think that every duffer I've ever met in the profession has worried me to find an engagement for her since I've been at the Pic!'

Mentally the girl on his knee was all at once a thousand leagues from him.

'You used to be such pals with Naomi!' he remonstrated.

'Oh, my dear boy!' She had her stuffy stop out again. '*I* like Naomi very well, but how can I take the responsibility of recommending a woman like that? She's not an artist.'

'She's not inspired,' admitted Tatham, 'but not many of them *are*. What is it she wants you to do?'

'Oh, the piece'll be going out in the autumn; she wants me to get her into the tour, she wants me to speak to Onslow for her; she wrote that she'd "be thankful for anything, even for half a, dozen lines". I believe she's in Queer Street... It's all very well –' She wrinkled her forehead and shrugged one shoulder. 'In my position, one can't *do* these things! I mean to say, how *can* I advise Onslow, or W. B., to take Naomi Knight?'

'I should have thought she could have played a small part quite as well as anybody else they're likely to get for the money,' he said drily. 'She has had plenty of experience.'

'Not in pieces like this; she hasn't the finish; they'll want it played in the same tone on the road as it's played at the Pic. Her manner's not West End enough. I mean to say, Naomi's all right in the No. 2 towns, and that sort of thing, but she hasn't got the style for first-class companies... It's a very difficult thing to say to her, of course, but' – her critical head was shaken ponderously – 'it's astonishing she doesn't see it for herself. 'Pon my word, it's extraordinary, the kind of people that go into the profession! the more one sees of it, the more extraordinary it is!'

When Naomi Knight arrived, a sadder and a shabbier figure than when he had last met her after the greetings had been exchanged and the feigned cheerfulness of the first few minutes was past – it was painful to Tatham to feel how sensitive the woman was to the girl's professional distance from her now. She had no hesitation in unveiling her necessities before him, and as she said deprecatingly, conscious of the suppliant's embarrassment, how 'grateful' she would be if Peggy would 'put in a word for her', his thoughts flashed back to the lodging over the dairy and refreshment rooms, where they used to call each other 'ducky', and romp.

She was a mediocre actress, but she loved her calling – loved it with her heart and her brain – and she was no longer young. When she explained that unless it yielded a pittance to her shortly, she would have to give it up and 'go in for something else', her recognition of the fact that her life had been a failure was not without pathos. She spoke vaguely of 'typewriting' or of 'dressmaking'. Though it appeared to him that it would be far wiser for her to quit the stage than to persist in the struggle to sustain a hand-to-mouth existence on it, she shrank from the final relinquishment of hope so pitiably, that the arrogance of the girl's attitude towards her jarred him as inhuman.

Peggy had not the faintest idea that she was being inhuman, nothing was further from her thoughts than to be or to sound unkind; she was merely actuated by a desire to parade her position, lest the other might fail to apprehend its splendours to the full. But every note in her voice was offensive, and the girl who had once boasted that she 'never forgot a pal' talked to the woman as she might have talked to a child.

'Well, as you ask my opinion,' she said, although it was not her opinion that had been asked, but her help, 'I'd strongly advise you to go in for anything you can – typewriting, dressmaking, whatever it is! I mean to say, supposing I did go to Onslow and say, "Look here, you've got to do this for *me*, she's a friend of mine – on the rocks – and she'll be all right in the part," supposing I did do it, what'd it amount to? What's the use of just one engagement? It wouldn't be a long one either – I mean to say, the only business the piece'll do'll be in the No. 1 towns; it won't play to the gas in the places where they're used to rough-and-tumble melodrama and that sort of thing – it'll be quite over their heads – it's much too clever and zoological. I see a very short tour for it, a very short tour. I told W. B. so frankly the other day. Well, in two or three months you'd be on your uppers! I mean to say, one can't – er – I couldn't *keep on* – I tell you honestly, my dear girl, I don't see any future for you in the profession! To make anything like a position today is most enormously difficult. You haven't a notion what hundreds of women there are – clever women, too, in their way – who'll never do any good.'

'Haven't I?' muttered Naomi.

'I tell you what it is, to come to the front on the stage today, a girl has got to be something quite out of the common. They want a lot! there's no doubt about it. There's so much ordinary talent knocking around that for a girl to come to the front today she's got to be different to anybody else, she's got to be able to –'

'She wasn't talking about "coming to the front"!' interrupted Tatham hotly. 'She'd be satisfied with a couple of pounds a week to go on with; wouldn't you, Miss Knight?'

'I'd take twenty-five shillings,' said the woman.

Peggy's gesture was intolerant. 'And that's just where it is! the profession's chock-a-block with actresses who're good enough for twenty-five shillings a week. They're the most difficult people in the world to do anything for!'

'I see your point,' said Naomi bitterly. 'I'm sorry I bothered you. It isn't always the geniuses that get to the front, though,' she added, turning to Tatham; 'a good many rotters get there – and a good many clever girls are too poor to afford to die in a sanatorium. You saw Elsie Lane was dead?'

He had not seen it; he gazed at her, startled.

'It's in *The Referee*. Of course, she'd been ill for years – consumption. I heard a little while ago she was starving; she tried as long as she could to hide how ill she was, but they say she looked so dreadful towards the end that she couldn't get an engagement at any money.'

'Is that so?' he murmured. The poignancy of it pierced him no less keenly because the tragedy was told in the hard, careless tones of a woman quivering under her own humiliation. He remembered his last glimpse of Elsie Lane, and cursed himself that he hadn't spoken to her. As vivid as his view of it in the Strand was his memory of the sick girl's painted face – painted, as he understood now, to mask the ravages of disease and enable her to earn her bread in the theatre. Farther back he looked, into a town whose name he had forgotten, and walked beside her through white, empty streets, and stood, wishing her 'luck' on a doorstep.

'There's a mention of me again in *The Ref*!' said Peggy, displaying a copy of the paper languidly. She pointed to a line in the Answers to Correspondents. 'Seen this, Naomi? "*Student of the Drama*: – Miss Peggy Harper's favourite flower is the lily of the valley."'

VII

When Theodosia told Tatham that she would like to retain the copy of *Shams* for a little while longer, she had said it with an audacious project her mind; and what passed between them subsequently, modified, but did not annul, the plan. She no longer dreamed of the delight of asking him to come to see her and proclaiming that a distinguished dramatic critic thought highly of comedy, but she did continue to think of begging a distinguished critic to read it, and to scribble an encouraging line on the subject if he found the comedy as meritorious as she expected him do.

Pritchard did not go to *The Aspect* office very often, and she had not been presented to him until she had been on the staff for two or three months. Since then, she had seen him several times. More than once he had sat on a table and talked to her – it was occasionally difficult to associate his diatribes on the paper with his simplicity on the table – and she did not think the amiable authority would refuse her petition if she showed herself conscious of asking a very great favour.

An opportunity for asking it was slow to arrive. But he did not refuse. Indeed, he consented at once, because he was under the impression that the play of her preamble had been written by herself. When she haltingly explained that it was by the author of *London Inside Out*, however, she became distressfully aware of a light of amusement in Mr Pritchard's eyes.

'You aren't going to be prejudiced against it, Mr Pritchard?' she pleaded. 'This is the man's *real* work – the kind of work he wants to do and always has done, excepting in that one wretched case. If I had had the courage, I'd have scratched his name off it before I showed it to you. Do read it –' She blundered to a breakdown.

'"Fairly"?' He peered at her, with a wry smile.

'I wasn't going to say "fairly",' she stammered, 'I was going to say "attentively".'

'I'll read it quite attentively enough to form an opinion,' he promised her. 'That's all right. But it won't advance Mr – er – Tatham in the slightest degree, you know, if I like it.'

An undesigned inflexion apprised her that few things were more improbable to his mind than that he would like it. And, as a matter of fact, his interest had abated so much that in the course of half an hour the roll that he was carrying was an object of aversion to him.

Many weeks passed before she heard his verdict, and her expectations had subsided considerably in the meanwhile.

'Well, I've read your friend's play, Miss Moore,' he announced hesitatingly. 'I can't say I think he has treated his subject in the happiest way.'

So much for her hope! She faltered, 'Oh?'

'I think it was bad judgment to make his hero a writing man. Why a writing man? Hasn't Mr Tatham heard of politicians, or inventors, or manufacturers, or engineers, or men in any other walk of life outside the arts? His purpose in *Shams* is to present an interesting study of a man's struggles to get on – and he puts the man in a profession that doesn't interest the public in the least. Short-sighted! To choose an author as the protagonist of an English play – or of an English novel – is to handicap the thing from the word "go"; no writer who knew his business would do it. What do you suppose the public care about somebody's difficulties in placing his manuscripts? If a dramatist or a novelist aims at awakening interest in the study of a career, it's folly for him to choose an artistic career – we aren't in France. In France it's done again and again, but in the land of good art and bad smells the public's tastes are infinitely better – and infinitely worse – than ours. Of course the French talk a very great deal more about *les économies* than about *les arts*, but for all that, above the level of apaches, Frenchmen who don't take any interest whatever in art and literature are even scarcer than Englishmen who do. Mr Tatham's a very acute observer, I'm surprised he doesn't recognise the limitations of the audience he's writing for.'

'Oh, you do think he shows observation?' she said eagerly. 'You don't think his work is – you find something to say for it, then?'

'I think very highly of his work,' replied Pritchard, in a key of protest, as if he had said so already. 'I think he lacks one very desirable quality – when I say 'desirable' I mean desirable for long runs – he lacks the so-called optimism that's always popular; he shows afflictions to be afflictions, instead of representing them as ultimate boons. If a nurse girl went mad and cut the baby's throat in a play of Mr Tatham's, we shouldn't be told at the end that the baby's parents, and the nurse girl's were filled with the peace of perceiving that all things worked mysteriously for some great and illuminative blessing. That's a mistake, commercially. No bland lie can be too preposterous to win wide approval. Say black is rose colour. Millions will smack their lips over the statement, and call the man who questions it a 'pessimist'. The national definition of a 'pessimist' is 'One who faces unwelcome facts.' 'Pessimist' and 'optimist' are the two most misused words in the English language. And, of course, *Shams* hasn't any titled personages in it. If Mr Tatham always writes about the middle classes I'm afraid he'll find that another commercial drawback.'

'You are,' faltered the girl, with more pride and happiness than she dared to show, 'taking Mr Tatham very seriously, aren't you?'

'Certainly I'm taking him very seriously. I'm bound to say I don't foresee his making a fortune in the theatre – though even that's largely a matter of luck — but I think he ought to make a big reputation. I want to send Shams to Onslow – I was talking to him about it the other day and he said he'd like to consider it.'

'Oh!' she gasped. 'But Mr Onslow refused it as "unsuitable" months ago!'

'That's irrelevant,' said Pritchard; 'this time he's going to read it. Of course he mayn't see any money in it. But if Onslow doesn't feel inclined to risk a production of it, it ought to be shown to somebody else – I'd like to see *Shams* get a chance somewhere. And anyhow,' he added, 'I think that he'll be quite sure to read anything that Mr Tatham sends to him in future.'

VIII

But as Theodosia felt that Tatham had made it impossible for her to correspond with him, and as it was equally out of the question for her to suggest to Mr Pritchard that he should do more than he had generously done, the author of *Shams* remained unaware that his prospects had an upward tendency. In this, his position differed widely from that of Peggy, who was conscious of being more valuable every day.

Her anticipations had been realised. Soon after she left the Piccadilly she had been offered an engagement at the Waterloo – and had asked for a contract at fifty pounds a week, and got it. She was not performing in the new part with so much seeming intelligence as she had performed in the part of 'Daphne' because the instruction afforded to her at the Waterloo, though patient and painstaking, had lacked the quality of inspiration; but she reproduced Forsyth's 'fetching and natural' smile with a tilted chin and her hands behind her back, and playgoers, having accepted her as delightful, continued to admire her. The management found it financially sound to put ten five-pound notes in an envelope every week for a girl who, troublesome though she was to teach, had the adherence of the Press and public. (Subsequent managements were equally complacent when she acquired the nerve to demand seventy-five pounds, and a hundred.) In the occupation which is given the most publicity – the calling in which an artist like Elsie Lane had suffered in want and died in squalor – this puppet had despotically 'arrived'.

And already the blare of the trumpets was duller to her ears – already she regarded homage as her birthright. She no longer enjoyed ecstatically, and wished, like a precocious child, that her delight were less. That childish wish had been the final impulse of a moribund simplicity. Keenly now she was alive to nothing but the immensity of her consequence in the social scheme. Diligently as she dwelt on every word of a complimentary criticism, she read the compliment, not with gratitude, but with a sense of her incomparable superiority to the scribes who praised her – if she knew nothing else about them, she knew that they were very poorly paid. Intellect impressed her not at all. Fame itself, other than histrionic fame, meant nothing to her. By this time the eminent men who had had the curiosity to approach her were fairly numerous, and their celebrity had not abashed her in the least – she too could boast celebrity; and as to the value of their achievements, she was too ignorant to be aware of it. She chatted to an R.A. and a Cabinet Minister with an unrestraint tinged by condescension. To an illustrious man of letters, whose name she had never heard before, she was rather rude.

It was not the girl's fault: she had been a good-natured, unpretentious little Cockney with a warm heart. It was the fault of the Cabinet Minister, the R.A., and the man of letters, of their wives and their daughters, and of a Press that pandered to an idolatry which it privately condemned: it was the fault, in fine, of the age in which she lived. Truly she believed – and London had conspired to persuade her – that the world of the theatre was the most important under Heaven; truly she believed that she shone effulgent in it by right of genius.

She could not escape the reflection that when she married a clerk she would be committing an act of sensational self-sacrifice. Alternately she was proud to think how generous she was, and surprised that poor old Chris didn't see for himself that it 'wouldn't do'. To be sure he had intimated something of the sort when she told him that her salary was to be fifty pounds a week, but he had allowed her to talk him over. In looking back, she was inclined to blame him for that, forgetting the nature of the protests she had made. If *she* were a man, she didn't think she'd find it good enough! But of course, Chris *was* weak. If he hadn't been weak, would he have stuck in a clerkship all these years ? Since he couldn't write plays, he should have done something else. What course had been open to him she did not profess to decide, but he should have buckled to! A concomitant of her inordinate self-esteem was, naturally, a lofty intolerance of failure.

She developed with rapidity an intolerance of many things – of restaurants that were not quite the smartest, and of any champagne that wasn't the 'only one worth drinking', though, of a truth, she could discover no difference between that and others, excepting under the prices on the wine list. Presents and invitations lost their novelty, and the chit who had felt important at the sight of a Clapham waiter opening her bottle of beer, was now airily familiar with what she called the 'meenew' of the Savoy. Not long since introduced to her first liqueur, she asserted listlessly that she 'always took green chartrooce'. She developed the habit of being late for appointments – when she contrived to remember them at all. Twice she had arranged with Tatham to meet her at the stage door, and dismissed him, after he had waited for twenty-five minutes in a draught, with the hurried explanation that 'some people had asked her to supper'.

But when, raging, he broke the engagement off, her better self, or her vanity, was wounded, and she did not approve his independence after all. Having cried and sulked for a week, she sent a little penitent letter to him, which made him feel that he was a brute for returning to her unwillingly.

It was about a fortnight after the reconciliation that one day, when he went to her in Keppel Street – Liverpool Road had been abandoned – he found her very natural and meek. She was nibbling a pencil forlornly, and struggling to write a description of her histrionic methods.

'Oh, I say!' she exclaimed, 'I am glad you've come in – I was going to drop you a postcard. *I* don't know how to do this beastly thing.'

He learnt that she had been petitioned to contribute to a series of articles that was appearing in *The Beholder*, under the heading, 'How I Study a Part.' In the present emergency her mother had proved useless, and the sight of a copy of the paper in which two columns of twaddle had been written, or signed, by Miss Clytie Pateward had increased her eagerness to figure in the series herself.

'Do you see?' she said. 'I'd have my photo in the middle, and my name printed three times. It'd be an awful pity to miss the ad! You might think of something for me, Chris. Have a cig, and tell me what to say.'

'What *have* you said?' he asked. 'How have you begun?'

'I've only done a little bit. "I study a part by first learning the lines, and then I work them up." That's all I've written so far.'

'That isn't much, is it?'

'Well, I don't know any more to say about it,' she said fretfully. 'I'm sick of the job – I've been sitting here for an hour!… I can't make out how Pateward's written such a lot. I've read it twice, but I can't say the same things that she does. I don't know what they've sent the rotten thing to me for – it's no help to me. Lot of flap, just to show how clever she is!'

'That's what *you've* got to do!'

'Well, I know all about that, but I'm an actress, I'm not an authoress… You might cut in and be useful,' she coaxed.

'Of course I will,' he said readily. 'I'm no good at it either, but I'll do what I can. Tell me how you do study a part. Then we'll make something of it between us; we'll try to dress it up and make it sound pretty.'

She regarded him open-mouthed, and her gaze wandered. For a cold, disquieting moment she realised that the way she 'studied' a part was to do in it exactly as she was told. For a moment only. 'There were some things too what-d'ye-call-it to be expressed!'

'Oh, well,' she faltered, 'I don't know just what I do. Look what my notices say!'

He nodded. He understood her better than her critics did.

'I suppose,' he sighed, 'that you might say that when you get a new part you lie awake all night thinking about it?'

'Oh yes,' she agreed; 'that's it!' She licked the pencil. '"I study a part by first learning the lines, and then I work them up, and then I lie awake all night –" No, that doesn't sound right! Oh, I say, do come on! It's giving me the hump.'

'I should begin differently. I should say – I should say that when a part is first handed to you, you feel… well, you feel awfully shy –'

'Shy?'

'Yes, "shy". You feel awfully shy, as if it were a stranger that you'd got to make friends with.'

'Do you think I ought to feel "shy"?' she demurred.

'Yes, yes,' he said impatiently; 'it's going to show how clever you are directly. You feel awfully shy, as if it were a stranger that you had to make friends with; and then, by degrees, you forget that it's a part – you seem to be speaking your own thoughts. In fact, you're not quite sure on the first night whether you're Peggy Harper, or the girl in the play… They'll lap that up.'

'Yes, that's the ticket!' she said. She scribbled for a few seconds, and contemplated a tangled sentence hopelessly. 'But how – where – which way do I start? Oh!' She flung the pencil in a tantrum across the room. 'Let it rip!… 'Tis a shame, 'tis a shame! You might do it *for* me — can't you do it *for* me, Chris? Do it at home for me, there's a dear! Do it for me at home, and bring it to me on Sunday. Do it for me by Sunday, and then you can come and read me what you've done. Won't you? I'd like to be in *The Beholder*. Do write it at home for me, Chris, there's a good chap!'

It was an easy matter to offer a suggestion, but a more difficult one to produce an article – which was the reason why very little of the non-sense in the 'How I Study a Part' series was written by the actors and actresses themselves. But by dint of taking a good deal of pains, since he was not a journalist, Tatham succeeded in producing that article 'By Miss Peggy Harper' which shed pleasure in so many English homes. He even took considerable interest in accomplishing it, although he was writing with his tongue in his cheek. Perhaps less for Peggy's sake than to humour his own taste, he sought to make this contribution the best that the series would contain. He toned down statements which on second thoughts appeared conceited; he invented emotions for her, and then deleted them. His efforts to steer a middle course between the egotistical and the colourless delayed him vastly.

But when he had finished fabricating her ingenuous confidences to the public, she sounded a little darling – her sweet simplicity was as delightful as her brilliant gifts.

It was not without a glow of satisfaction that he bore his work to her on Sunday. A postcard urging him to come to middle-day dinner, and 'bring that thing with him', had reached him the previous afternoon, and he had replied by telegram that he wouldn't fail.

A taxi-cab was waiting before the house, and the sitting room was empty when he entered it. But he heard her voice and her mother's behind the folding doors. Peggy came in swiftly. She had on a hat, and was plainly pressed for time. Her white blouse, fastened at the throat with a brooch depicting a couple of tennis rackets, was sprinkled with various bits of cheap jewellery which her means had permitted her recently to acquire. Under the rackets, a wish-bone, a turquoise horse-shoe, and a bedizened safety-pin were followed by a pendant pro-claiming that her Christian name began with a P. Westward, a watch hung. To the North-east, a silver insect, with amethyst wings, would have been solitary but for a 'Chaste design, set with fine quality pearls, at £1 10s A yard or two of chain encircling her neck became a loop line to a true-lover's knot of red enamel before its terminus in a bunch of charms at her waist.

'Oh, I say, I'm awfully sorry, but I've got to go out,' she said carelessly. 'Mother's not going, you'll stop just the same.' Her glance fell on the article. 'Is that it? I haven't got time to look at it now – I must bolt.'

By the whitening of his face it was revealed to her that he was very angry. To justify herself, she explained, with a quick frown:

'I'm going to lunch with Dicker, the airman.'

'Dicker be damned,' said Tatham quietly. 'Where you're concerned, I don't play second fiddle to Dicker, or anyone else. I'm tired of it... I thought we had settled all this once and for all?'

'Yes – well, I've changed my mind,' she said.

'I haven't changed mine,' said he.

'Think I'm going to let everything slide to please *you*?' Her voice was high. 'I've got something else to think about, I give you *my* word! What next? One'd think you were I don't know what!'

Something, the protrusion of a surly mouth, the timbre of the coarse defiance, jerked his remembrance to an afternoon when her mother had reviled him.

'I'm the man you're engaged to marry. And while we *are* engaged, you've got to count me "first". If that isn't good enough, the engagement isn't good enough.'

'"Good enough"!' she cried derisively. 'Crumbs! don't make me laugh, I've got a cracked lip.'

After a moment Tatham said, trembling: 'You'd better make haste – your taxi's outside, ticking away twopences.'

Behind the folding doors, which had been imperfectly closed, Betsy Harper sat rocking with pleasure on a trunk.

IX

In the sunlight of a morning four years later Christopher Tatham was absorbed by the task of transferring lobelia from the pots in which it had arrived to the soil of a circular flowerbed. And the earth smelt good to him. It was one of those fair, allusive mornings when the garden of a semi-detached villa is not one rod, pole, or perch smaller than the imagination of the tenant, and the labourer was feeling that his limited lawn extended as far as the heart of Nature. It was one of those mornings when the suburban house-holder bustles for his train with a wistful glance at the verdure behind his gate; and the author, whose breakfast-room window had afforded a view of neighbours bustling for their trains, paused in his occupation of planting lobelia, to realise anew that he need never go to the City any more.

The thought was wonderfully arresting, and the flowerpots lay neglected.

'Slacking?' laughed Theodosia. She herself was very indolent, in a basket chair under a laburnum tree, with an illustrated paper on her lap. 'There are some sugar-plums for you in this week's number,' she said; 'and there's a picture of a lady you used to know.'

'Theo, something's happened – I need never go to the City any more!'

'That's lovely!' she smiled. 'When did you find it out – today, or three years ago?'

'Just this minute – all over again!'

Her gaze deepened. He loitered closer to her.

'I believe you'd rather have been a gardener than anything else,' she told him.

'Oh, writing's not bad sometimes… You don't care for it as you did?'

She reflected. 'I've so much else to care for now,' she explained happily.

'I wonder if *he'll* write?' said Tatham. 'I don't want him to.'

'I don't know *what* I want Baby to be.'

'Not a writing-man… We shall soon have to leave off calling him "Baby", shan't we?'

'Oh, there's time enough!' she cooed.

'I shouldn't like the Bar for him,' declared the father, after a pause, remembering his own father.

'Nor the Church,' said she, thinking of hers... 'I don't know why you should mind his writing, though; *you've* nothing to complain of now – unless you're eager for thousands a year?'

'I don't know that thousands a year are very necessary,' he murmured. 'You and he, that's the kind of thing that really matters to a man. I've everything I want... Show me the sugar-plums in the paper – I'm always grateful for my sugar-plums.'

'Look at the picture first!' she said.

It was a picture of a girl in a reefer and a pilot cap, smiling, with a tilted chin, and her hands behind her back. Under it was printed: 'Miss Peggy Harper, whose engagement to Lord Capenhurst, was recently announced. Like her fiancé, Miss Harper has always been devoted to yachting.'

'It's a funny world,' said Tatham thoughtfully.

For a space they were silent, looking back – marvelling at the minuteness of big things past... The strangeness of their being here together swayed them both; for an instant the suburban garden held all the mystery of life. Both reviewed a love that had been an exquisite illusion: The man was conscious that the woman by his side was far removed from the girl whom he had idealised: the woman knew that her husband was a world away from the lover of whom she used to dream... In the contentment of a perfect understanding they turned to each other and their hands touched.

'Hark!' he exclaimed, alarmed.

'He's crying!' gasped Theodosia.

The paper fell on the grass as they ran upstairs to Baby.

BIOGRAPHICAL NOTE

Leonard Miller was born in Belsize Park in London. He studied to be a solicitor in England and then went on to study law in Germany. His father's financial troubles forced him into work however and he became an overseer at a diamond mine in Kimberley, South Africa. Having returned to London in the late 1880s, he began a career as an actor and actor-manager and took Leonard Merrick as a stage name. (He was later to change his name legally to Merrick too.)

Merrick wrote his first novel *Mr Bazalgette's Legacy* in 1888 and, though it was not a success, he persevered nonetheless. After spending time in America and Paris, Merrick married in 1894 (his wife and their daughter would both predecease him). Merrick went on to write a number more novels, plays and short stories which touched on psychological, detective and romantic genres. Merrick's work was held in high esteem by his contemporaries; in 1918 'The Works of Leonard Merrick' was published, a collection of fifteen volumes selected and introduced by illustrious authors of the era (G.K. Chesterton, H.G. Wells, J.M. Barrie amongst others). In fact, J.M. Barrie famously referred to Merrick as a 'novelist's novelist'; his reputation has suffered somewhat in subsequent years but several of his works have been adapted for film and television.

Merrick died in a nursing home in London on 7th August 1939.